'I can't think why you came to this primitive island, but I'm going to find out.' Dr Alexander Capodistrias was obviously puzzled that Sister Nicole Langley had come all the way from London to work on a remote Greek island. And in her turn Nicole found the surgeon a complete enigma!

Margaret Barker trained as a State Registered Nurse at a large hospital in the North of England. Soon afterwards, she married a graduate from the nearby university and they have recently celebrated thirty happy years of marriage. They have two sons and a daughter, and one grandchild. Their work has taken them to America, Africa, Asia and Europe, and this has given Margaret ideas for the books which she has set overseas; her own teaching hospital has provided the background for her English stories. She and her husband now live in a sixteenth-century thatched cottage near the sea.

OLYMPIC SURGEON

BY

MARGARET BARKER

MILLS & BOON LIMITED
15–16 BROOK'S MEWS
LONDON W1A 1DR

*All the characters in this book have no existence outside
the imagination of the Author, and have no relation
whatsoever to anyone bearing the same name or names.
They are not even distantly inspired by any individual
known or unknown to the Author, and all the incidents
are pure invention.*

*The text of this publication or any part thereof may
not be reproduced or transmitted in any form or by any
means, electronic or mechanical, including photo-
copying, recording, storage in an information retrieval
system, or otherwise, without the written permission
of the publisher.*

*This book is sold subject to the condition that it shall not,
by way of trade or otherwise, be lent, resold, hired out or
otherwise circulated without the prior consent of the
publisher in any form of binding or cover other than that
in which it is published and without a similar condition
including this condition being imposed on the subsequent
purchaser.*

*First published in Great Britain 1986
by Mills & Boon Limited*

© Margaret Barker 1986

*Australian copyright 1986
Philippine copyright 1986*

ISBN 0 263 75482 0

Set in 10 on 11½ pt Linotron Times
03–0886–53,300

*Photoset by Rowland Phototypesetting Limited
Bury St Edmunds, Suffolk
Made and printed in Great Britain by
William Collins Sons & Co. Limited, Glasgow*

CHAPTER ONE

NICOLE hurried through the narrow cobbled street, picking her way over the ancient, uneven stones. A tiny old Greek woman, shrouded in black, paused in mid-sweep to lean on her broom and watch the young English girl dash past. She was waiting for the usual friendly greeting, but there was no cheerful *'Kaliméra'* this morning. The old woman frowned as she watched the distracted figure run up the path to the old pharmacy.

I thought so; she must be ill—I'm not surprised; very strange, these foreigners always rushing about—and in this heat too.

The pharmacy door was open, but there was no-one inside. Nicole walked nervously round the big square room, looking at the ornate antique jars on the shelves. Belladonna, Cantharides; the labels were hand-painted on the pottery. How quaint; but this couldn't still be used as a surgery, could it? And where was the old doctor who was supposed to be here every morning?

There was a movement behind her, and she turned to see a tall man standing in an alcove. The bright sunlight, shining into the pharmacy, had momentarily blinded her, and it was difficult to focus on the man in the shadows.

'I was looking for Dr Capodistrias . . .' she began.

The man crossed the room and stood in front of her. 'I am Dr Capodistrias.'

Nicole stared up at him in amazement. The deep, mellow voice was not what she had expected. And he was much too young—couldn't be more than thirty-five. 'But you can't be . . .'

He laughed at her confusion, and she found herself fascinated by the wide, sensual mouth and strong white teeth.

'I'm Alexander Capodistrias. You were expecting to see my father, Demetrius. He's ill, so I'm taking care of things. What can I do for you?'

Nicole held out her hand, with its hastily improvised bandage. 'I'd like you to . . .'

'Come into the surgery,' Dr Capodistrias cut in.

She followed the tall figure through the alcove into a cool, interior room with no windows. He motioned her to sit down as he placed himself on a chair in front of her, and took hold of her bandaged hand.

Nicole watched the long, tapering fingers removing the strips of cloth, and, in spite of her agitation, found herself enjoying the attentions of this handsome doctor. He was so good-looking! Rather like a Greek god, descended from Mount Olympus on to this little island of Ceres. But how unexpected to find someone like this—so distinguished-looking, so debonair! And he speaks English like a native, she thought.

The deep wound on her finger was now revealed, and he raised his face to look at her. Although her hand was throbbing painfully, she couldn't help noticing the brilliant green of his eyes—or were they hazel? The two colours seemed to have merged into a dazzling unique shade of their own.

'How did it happen?' His voice was brusque, no-nonsense, authoritarian.

'I was bitten by a cat,' she replied, evenly.

'You were *what*?' he thundered.

She repeated her statement, but with a little less confidence.

'Of all the stupid females! What on earth were you doing?'

'I was trying to rescue it,' Nicole defended.

'From what? Cats on this island are very self-sufficient.'

'It had been crying all night in the ruins of the old villa next to mine.' She was trying to sound calm, but inwardly she was fuming. The doctor's domineering attitude was the last thing she wanted. 'I thought it was trapped under a stone or something, so I went in to see if I could release it. It was hidden in some thick bushes, and when I put my hand in, it bit me,' she finished.

'Of course it bit you! It was probably terrified of you. What an idiotic thing to do! How big was this cat?'

Nicole paused and took a deep breath. 'It was only a kitten. I was hoping to take it back to its mother . . .'

The doctor's rich, deep laughter drowned her voice. Humiliated though she felt, she still found the sound exciting, almost thrilling. Her nerves were strained with the tension between them.

'I'd better get you patched up,' he said nonchalantly, reaching for a bottle of Betadine.

As he cleaned the wound, the unnerving feel of his soothing fingers helped to anaesthetise the pain. She watched mutely as he bandaged the finger, tightly and expertly.

'I'm not going to put a stitch in it,' he told her. 'It should be okay if you keep it tightly wrapped. I'll have to give you an anti-tetanous injection, of course, and I'll see you again in a few days. When do you go home?'

'I'm staying for a year. I've come to work here.'

'Really? Doing what?'

'I'm a nursing sister,' she replied quietly. 'I've come out to take charge of the new hospital.'

'Ye gods! I don't believe it! Not you! But you can't

even put a bandage on. That dirty old bit of tea-towel
you'd wrapped . . .'

'When you've just been bitten by a wild animal, you
grab the first thing you can find!' Nicole was close to
tears.

'Let's get the injection over and then we can talk.
Bend over that couch,' he said unceremoniously as he
turned his back to prepare the syringe.

She leaned over the couch, fumbling with the belt
around her waist. This was awful! She felt his hand on
the back of her shorts.

'Come on, girl! This is no time to be coy. I can't give an
injection through all that cotton,' Alexander said
impatiently.

She pulled the shorts down to the required level and
waited for the expected stab of pain. After a few
seconds, she heard him moving around behind her.

'It's okay. You can get dressed; I've finished.' He was
rinsing out the syringe before placing it in the ancient
autoclave.

Nothing disposable here, Nicole noticed, some of it
was positively nineteenth century. What a place for a
man like this to work! She fastened her leather belt
tightly, wishing she'd had time to put on her new shorts.
These old things were terribly baggy, and it would have
been nice to make an impression on this very attractive
doctor.

'Come through to the office.' He spoke like a man who
was used to instant obedience.

Nicole followed him into a small room at the front of
the building. She saw a desk, crowded with papers,
boxes of pills, unopened envelopes, and thought, I don't
see why he should chide me about inefficiency.

As if reading her mind, Alexander waved a hand
impatiently over the desk. 'I've only just taken over

from my father. This is going to need some re-organisation. That's where you come in.'

She stared across the desk into the brilliant green-hazel eyes. 'But I'm still on holiday. I don't start until next week . . .' she protested.

'Correction; you start today. We've been trying to get in touch with you in London. No-one knew where you were. I'd no idea you were on the island. How long have you been here?'

'A week. I wanted some time to relax and get acclimatised before I started work.'

'Well, the holiday's over. Anyway, you look as if you've had your fair share of the sun.' His eyes swept appraisingly over the slender brown legs beneath the brief pink shorts.

Her hands moved defensively to cover her thighs, feeling suddenly that her dress was decidedly unsuitable.

'Put this on,' he ordered, tossing Nicole a white coat. 'We'll go down to the hospital when we've finished morning surgery, and they'll kit you out with your uniform. How does your finger feel now?'

It was the first time he'd shown any compassion towards her. 'It's fine,' she lied, trying to ignore the steady, painful throbbing.

'Good.' He was rifling through the desk drawers. 'I'm trying to find your papers. My father said . . . Ah, here we are. Sister Nicole Langley; age twenty-five; ward sister from Benington General. What made you want to come out here?' Alexander asked suddenly.

She met his searching gaze unflinchingly, having anticipated the question over and over again in her mind. 'I think it's very easy to settle into a rut in a large teaching hospital. One tends to forget all the advantages of having modern scientific equipment. Out here it will be something of a challenge,' Nicole answered. She wasn't going to tell him the real reason.

'Oh, come on, you can do better than that,' the doctor snapped, irritated by her evasive answer. 'Stop pussy-footing around with me, my girl . . .'

'I'm not your girl, Doctor, and if we are to work together, I would be grateful if you would use a little professional etiquette. Where I come from, we're used to certain standards . . .'

'I'm sure you are.' He was grinning broadly now. 'It must be wonderful to work in London—or even just outside London, at the Benington. Tell me about it, Sister.'

Something about his bantering tone put her on her guard. 'Have you ever been to England?' she asked warily.

'You could say that,' he smiled. 'I went to school there, and I trained in London. In fact I was there only last week.'

Capodistrias, of course! This must be the famous consultant from St Celine's. She'd heard about him so often. Oh, my God! And she'd been using her patronis-ing tone. 'I'm sorry, sir. I didn't realise who you were. But surely someone else could have taken over here. I mean . . . your work in London . . .'

'Don't remind me,' he muttered darkly. 'Family is family here in Greece. When my father had a coronary, I flew straight out. My registrar has taken over at St Celine's until my return.'

'Is your father in the hospital here?'

'No, we're nursing him over at the family home in Symborio Bay. He's recovering well.'

'I'm so glad. There's just one more thing . . .'

'Yes?' He looked across the desk and studied the fine-boned intense face, thinking what sensitive blue eyes she had.

'Is there any danger of rabies—I mean, from my cat-bite?' she faltered.

'There hasn't been a case of rabies in these islands for forty years.' His voice was icy and his eyes blazed angrily. 'Don't you think I would have commenced innoculation if it had been otherwise? What do you take me for?'

I take you for a self-opinionated, male chauvinistic pig, but I'm not going to say it, Nicole thought. She remained silent for a few moments, trying to calm the inner turmoil. It would be a mistake to get on the wrong side of her boss. She raised her eyes to meet his with a cool stare. 'What would you like me to do first, Dr Capodistrias?' she asked quietly.

'Well, as we don't seem to have any patients here at the moment, you could make a start on . . .'

'Ghiatro, ghiatro!'

Through the window, Nicole could see a small, dark man running up the path, calling for the doctor. It sounded urgent.

Alexander Capodistrias leapt to his feet and went to meet him. They conversed rapidly in Greek. Nicole's knowledge of the language was inadequate, and she waited patiently for the doctor to explain.

'His wife's in labour,' he said briefly at the end of the interrogation. 'We'll have to go.' He was already checking the contents of a dark leather bag. 'I take it you're midder-trained.'

'Yes, but . . .'

'No time for buts. Come on,' Alexander urged.

They were half-way down the path when Nicole gestured to the wide-open door. 'Shouldn't we lock up or something?' she asked anxiously.

'The Greeks are a very honest race,' he answered patiently. 'I can't vouch for the tourists, but there aren't many around yet. We never lock anything at home.'

The father-to-be was hurrying ahead through the twisty, twiny streets, turning from time to time, his eyes beseeching them to hurry. Eventually they reached his house, which opened directly on to the rough cobblestones. The cool interior was welcome after the rising heat of the mid-morning sun.

When her eyes became accustomed to the comparative darkness, Nicole could see a young girl lying in a large bed, surrounded by several older women who were nodding and chatting volubly to each other. One of the women, dressed in black, seemed to be in charge of the proceedings. She was standing at the foot of the bed, and from her urgent tone it was obvious she was exhorting the poor girl to push.

'I think we'll get rid of the spectators,' Alexander Capodistrias said under his breath. He raised his voice, uttered a few well chosen words in Greek, and the room cleared as if by magic. Only the old woman in charge remained. She eyed the newcomers warily, resenting the intrusion.

The doctor examined his patient, talking to her reassuringly all the time. When he had finished, he turned to Nicole.

'She's been in labour for some time. The waters have broken and we've got a breech presentation.'

Nicole drew in a sharp breath. 'Can't we take her down to the hospital?'

'Not unless we put her on the back of a donkey, or carry her down the steps,' he replied dryly. 'Up here in the old town, we've got no modern transport. We'll have to deliver her here. Apparently, she wasn't due for another two weeks, otherwise we'd have had her in the hospital.' He turned back to smile at the young girl who was looking anxious at the prolonged consultation, and spoke gently to her in Greek.

Several minutes passed, during which Nicole palpated the patient's abdomen for any visible signs of contractions. 'The uterine contractions seem to be ineffective, sir,' she reported after a while.

'I agree.' He was scrubbing his hands and arms at the tiny sink in the corner of the room.' Get the Oxytocin from my bag, Sister. We'll have to induce the baby.'

Nicole prepared the required amount, and Dr Capodistrias administered it intravenously. When the expected contractions started to come Nicole helped the mother, while the doctor tried to manoeuvre the baby into a deliverable position. Nicole could see the tiny buttocks at the head of the birth canal. She had hurriedly boiled up the forceps, but was praying that they wouldn't need them. The buttocks were wedged, unable to emerge any further.

'Scalpel, Sister.' The doctor's voice was perfectly controlled.

Nicole handed over the sterile instrument, and he made a swift incision in the perineum. The infant started to slide out backwards; the legs appeared, then the arms and shoulders, and at last came the head. He took the baby into his arms and placed it on the young mother's abdomen.

'It's a girl!' Nicole never ceased to be amazed at the miracle of a new life.

Tears of joy were running down the mother's face as she reached for her child. The young father was sitting on the bed, his arm round his wife.

They can't be more than nineteen or twenty, thought Nicole, suddenly feeling that twenty-five was over the hill. Would she ever have a family of her own? Probably not, now. One long engagement was bad enough—too much hassle—and marriage would be even worse.

'It's a good thing we got here when we did.' The
doctor's voice was stern as he glanced at the old woman
returning to the bedside, fortunately unaware of his
disapproval. 'This is the sort of thing we're up against
out here. Lack of knowledge, lack of equipment, lack of
training . . . I could go on, but I won't. My father built
the new hospital, but we still have problems getting the
patients there.' He sounded exasperated.

'Never mind. You saved this one.' Nicole's blue eyes
were full of admiration. 'If you hadn't come, she'd have
been just one more statistic.'

He nodded. 'Thank you for your help, Sister.'

She smiled. 'Let's not rest on our laurels, sir. We'd
better go to work on the after-birth.'

'Exactly.' He turned again to the patient, bending his
broad back, and she thought what a desirably sensual
man he was. But she wasn't going to get involved with
him. He was the same type as Clark.

The baby cried lustily as Nicole cleaned and bathed
her, before wrapping her in a blanket. She noted, with
relief, that she was a good colour. 'What about post-
natal care?' she asked briskly.

'In a couple of hours the mother'll be fit to go down the
steps as far as the new road. I'll telephone for the
ambulance to meet us there. She can ride on one of the
donkeys.'

'Really?' Nicole's voice conveyed her amazement.

'As I said, we have a few transport problems on the
island,' the doctor snapped irritably. 'The streets up
here in the old town are too narrow for motorised
vehicles. The ambulance from the hospital can only get
within two hundred steps of this part. There's nothing
we can do about it. Go and have a couple of hours off
duty,' he finished abruptly. 'And change out of that

awful white coat. It does nothing for you. You'd look better in a sack.'

Nicole glanced down at the stained overall, dismayed at his disapproval of her appearance. How dare he criticise her! She hadn't expected to be out all day on an errand of mercy. With a start, she realised she hadn't even had time for breakfast, her finger was hurting her, and it was already late in the afternoon.

'Come back about six. I'll hold the fort until then. The old lady can help me, if necessary.' His peremptory tone dismissed her, as if she were a junior nurse in training.

Nicole turned and went out into the hot sunshine, not trusting herself to reply. Keeping in the shady part of the street, she made her way back to the villa and pushed open the heavy door leading to the small courtyard. Narrow, uneven stone steps took her up to the studio apartment on the top floor. She paused to catch her breath after the climb, and looked out from the large stone patio across the picturesque red roof-tops towards the sea. It was a mind-blowing view which never ceased to amaze her.

The sea changed colour, continuously, as it mirrored the moods of the sky. Tiny fishing vessels rippled across the smooth surface of the water, and up on the green hillsides the sheep and goats meandered aimlessly as they cropped the grass. She could hear the soft tinkling of their bells, and smell the pungent aroma of oregano. It was only a few hours since she had left the apartment, but it seemed like days.

She opened the little door and went into the living area. The maid had been in to clean, and everything looked spick and span. She must have polished the tiled floor again, and shaken the coloured, woven mats. Nicole went up the two steps into the bedroom, and stripped off her clothes, flinging them on the bed in distaste as she remembered the doctor's unflattering remarks.

The water in the shower was hot, and she luxuriated in its soothing cascade. It was a pity the shower hadn't been fixed to the wall; Nicole had to hold it in one hand, while rubbing shampoo in with the other and trying not to spray outside the tiny shower cubicle. Greek plumbing required the expertise of a contortionist, she decided.

She fluffed out her fair hair, wrapped herself in a towel, and went to sit on the patio to catch the last rays of the sun. Mmm! She already loved this place. Everyone had told her she was mad to take a studio up in the old town—too many steps! But it would be good to get away from hospital in her off-duty. She wanted to have some time to herself; time to think about the future and what she was going to do with herself, now that she had broken off her engagement and Clark had gone to the States without her.

Funny, I don't feel the least bit sad now that I'm out here, she thought. I should have had the courage to split up ages ago. Two years was too long to be engaged to an ambitious ego-maniac like Dr Clark Richards.

There was a movement in the bushes of the ruined villa next door. The wild kitten that had bitten her was meekly clambering over some rough stones, in hot pursuit of a large mother cat. Every few steps the mother turned to chide her offspring, and the plaintive cries rose up to Nicole. Thank goodness for that, she thought. At least I won't be wakened again by the kitten crying all night.

She glanced down at her finger. It had stopped throbbing. The doctor was right; it had been a stupid thing to do, but he needn't have been quite so horrible about it! A little kindness doesn't cost anything, Nicole thought.

He could have talked soothingly to me, like he spoke to the young mother, instead of jumping down my throat like that. She remembered the tender voice he'd used during the delivery. If he were to speak to me like that . . .

Pull yourself together! You're like a love-sick teenager! Just because you've considered yourself virtually married for the past two years, you don't have to go over-board for the first man you see, even if he is rather gorgeous. He's only a man—and an arrogant one at that. Exactly the same type as Clark, come to think of it; yes—autocratic, self-centred, ambitious. Steer clear of him at all costs! I'll spend a year out here, gaining experience of medicine in a primitive environment, and then I'll move on somewhere else. The world's my oyster, now that I'm free!

Dr Capodistrias was plainly surprised at Nicole's transformation when she returned to the little house. It wasn't that she had tried too hard—no, she had gone for understated chic in her choice of a cool white cotton dress, with a deliberately formal collar and neckline at the front, and a cut-away section at the back, which revealed her newly acquired tan. He looked hot and tired as he handed her the newborn infant.

'You look refreshed,' he commented. 'I'm glad one of us was able to take a break.'

She smiled up at him. 'I came back as soon as I could, sir.' Best not to antagonise him. The baby stirred in her arms, and she wrapped the blanket round her.

There was a commotion outside the door as the donkey arrived, and the women gathered once more to see the baby. Nicole marvelled at the ease with which the young mother sat, side-saddle, on the docile beast. She looked like a schoolgirl going off on a picnic. It was impossible to believe that only a couple of hours ago she had been in the throes of a difficult labour.

The strange procession made its way down the kali strata, as the main street was called. Nicole found it difficult to ward off the prying fingers of the friendly people, intent on touching the new baby. She was polite, but firm, as she held the baby close to her. The journey took only a few minutes, but Nicole was immensely relieved to leave the antiquated street behind. When she saw the new road stretching in front of her, and stepped into the waiting ambulance, it was like returning to the twentieth century from a bygone age.

CHAPTER TWO

THE ambulance tore down the new road at break-neck speed, as if its descent was a matter of life and death. Nicole held the baby tightly in her arms and smiled reassuringly at the young mother. The deep blue of the harbour seemed to be rushing to meet them as they encircled the bay.

Through the windows, Nicole could see the early-evening activity along the waterfront. The crew of a sponge boat were busily beating and washing sponges; two men had placed a basket of live lobsters outside one of the tavernas and were beginning to haggle over the price with the owner. A few early-season tourists merged with the locals at the harbour-side tables, sipping ouzo while they watched the sunset.

The ambulance drove up the short stretch of road from the harbour, grinding to a halt outside the hospital. Nicole breathed a sigh of relief that they had made it. Motorised transport was such a new phenomenon on the island that there were few, if any, road regulations. The two island taxis and the ambulance drove straight down the centre of the narrow road, and it was a case of get-out-of-the-way-or-else! The island policeman smiled benignly over the top of his ouzo glass as the vehicles jockeyed for position along the harbour, where the sides of the road were completely unprotected from the deep water. Nicole wondered how long it would be before some tragedy spoiled their illusory calm.

She clambered out of the ambulance and stood back to admire the new edifice. It was a long, low, stone building, painted white. In the traditional style of Ceres, it blended in well with the ancient architecture around it. If, as she understood to be correct, Dr Demetrius Capodistrias had financed the whole project, then he must be an exceedingly rich man.

She went in through the wide main entrance to a cool reception area. A fan was whirring noisily in the ceiling overhead. Obviously air-conditioning would be too much of an anachronism for the island. A small, plump nurse in a light blue uniform came hurrying across the tiled floor to greet them.

'Sister Langley, welcome to Ceres Hospital. I'm Staff Nurse Ariadne Stangos.'

Nicole detected only a slight Greek accent, as she took the nurse's outstretched hand. 'Thank you. I'm looking forward to working here.'

'And this must be the newborn infant we've been waiting for.' The staff nurse reached out her plump brown arms to take the baby from Nicole. Her smile broadened as she raised her eyes to a point behind Nicole's head. 'Dr Capodistrias, I was hoping you would come because I need . . .'

'Yes, yes, Staff Nurse,' he interrupted abruptly. 'I'm sure you need lots of things, but unless it's desperately urgent, *I* need a long cold drink. I've been stuck up there in the old town since early morning . . .'

'Of course, sir; I'm sorry. And you too, Sister; you must be tired . . .'

Nicole opened her mouth to say something, but Staff Nurse Stangos was in full conversational flight.

'I'll take care of the new admissions while you two relax. You know your way to the staff common room, sir.' The staff nurse was unable to disguise the pride in her voice when she mentioned this amenity.

Alexander Capodistrias gave a tired smile. 'Of course

I do.' He put his hand lightly under Nicole's arm. 'This way, Sister.'

The touch of his fingers was light and brief, but she reacted as if it had been an electric shock.

'I didn't mean to startle you.' He looked down at her with amusement in his green-hazel eyes, and, to her annoyance, she blushed.

They walked a few steps along a corridor which seemed to span the length of the hospital, before turning into a spacious room that looked out over the sea. Nicole went over to the long windows and out on to the verandah.

'It's beautiful!' she breathed, as she looked across the blue water to the green and brown hill, dotted with white houses, on the opposite side of the bay.

'Yes, we're rather pleased with it.' Alexander had come up behind her and was standing too close for comfort. He would surely be able to hear her heart pounding noisily. What on earth was the matter with her? She put a hand on the iron rail to steady herself.

'We could have our drinks out here,' he said, motioning towards one of the tables.

Nicole moved across and sat down thankfully. When she raised her eyes, the doctor was studying her intently.

'I can't think why you came to this primitive island, but I'm going to find out,' he said softly.

'I've given you my reason, Doctor.'

He gave her a teasing smile, and shook his head. 'Not good enough, Sister.'

'I think it's none of your business.'

Her words sounded braver than she felt, but his answer was uncharacteristically meek. 'You're quite right; we're both here to do a job, so let's get on with it.' His tone was brisk and efficient. 'But first, that drink. Dominic!'

'Yes, sir.' A young man in a white shirt and black trousers came hurrying through an alcove and across the room.

'I'll have a cold beer, and Sister will have . . . ?'

'A fruit juice, please,' Nicole said.

'Certainly.' Dominic disappeared again.

Nicole turned to her companion. 'Who's that?'

'He's a young man who's waiting to go to medical school, and he's worth his weight in gold. He spends all his time at the hospital, studying, and we give him a small wage for the odd jobs he does. His parents work at the house.'

'The house?'

'My father's house. Dominic was born there. His mother is our cook,' Alexander explained.

The young Greek had returned and was setting the drinks on the table with a flourish. 'Will that be all, sir?'

'Yes, thank you, Dominic. How's the studying coming along?'

'Very well. I was working on it just now.'

'Well, go back to it, then. Don't waste time; it's such a precious commodity.' Alexander was smiling as he said this, and the young man's eyes shone with admiration, as he looked at the famous consultant.

'His English is excellent,' Nicole said, when he had gone.

'Should be; he had an excellent teacher,' Alexander said with a grin.

Staff Nurse Stangos came bustling in as they were finishing their drinks. 'Are you ready to do a round, sir?'

He groaned. 'What a slave driver you are, Ariadne.'

Nicole noticed the use of the first name and wondered when he would use hers. He was obviously puzzled by her, just as she found him to be a complete enigma. It was utterly incongruous to have such an eminent surgeon out here, on this unsophisticated island, even if it was his birthplace. He must be terribly fond of his father to leave his position in London.

'Perhaps Sister Langley would like to come round too . . .' Nurse Stangos began tentatively.

'Oh, I think it's imperative.' The doctor's tone brooked no refusal. 'The sooner we get her into harness, the better.'

He was very much the important consultant as he swept along the corridor, and Nicole smiled as she watched the reaction of his patients. He called in to see every one of them, and they plainly adored and respected him. Towards the end of the round she had lost count of the patients they had seen, and asked Nurse Stangos to remind her.

'Basically, there are twenty beds at the moment, but we are going to expand, as the need arises. We take all but the most complicated surgical cases, but now that Dr Capodistrias is here, everything is possible.' She smiled up at the eminent surgeon.

'Not quite.' They were standing in the small operating theatre, and the doctor was surveying the equipment with a critical eye. 'I would hesitate to perform delicate heart surgery here, without a full back-up team, an intensive care unit . . . Need I go on?' He waved an arm expansively. 'And I don't think Sister is qualified in that direction, are you?'

'No, but . . .'

'Exactly. We'll cope with general medicine, and minor surgical operations, but the difficult cases will have to go to the mainland, as they've always done.'

He turned his back on Nicole and walked out into the corridor. She followed, quietly fuming, wanting to retort that you couldn't specialise in everything, that she had held down a demanding post as medical ward sister for a whole year, and before that she had . . .

'Is something troubling you, Sister?' Alexander's brilliantly perceptive eyes were boring into her.

She met his gaze without flinching. 'Of course not. I'd like to see the new mother and baby now.' Her voice was cool and professional.

'Certainly. Obstetrics this way.' He strode along to the end of the corridor and pushed open a swing door.

There were three mothers in the room, with their babies, the beds separated from each other by partitions, open to the central area. A young Greek nurse was helping the new mother with her baby.

'This is Nurse Vlasto, Sister,' said the staff nurse.

The young nurse smiled at the new sister, thinking how pretty she looked, and feeling relieved to see that she was quite young. She smiled provocatively at Dr Capodistrias but he didn't notice her. He never did. I might as well be a machine for all the attention I get, she thought. Perhaps when I'm older and more important he might look at me. She sighed, and turned back to help the mother.

Nicole went closer to the bedside, to observe how the infant was breast feeding. The baby's mouth was firmly closed and she appeared to be asleep. 'Has she been feeding long?' she asked Nurse Vlasto.

'She hasn't taken much, Sister.'

Nicole bent down and stroked the baby's cheek gently for a few seconds. The tiny eyes opened and the little rosebud mouth moved from side to side.

'Let's try her again,' Nicole urged, as she lifted the baby's head towards the mother's breast. This time the baby took the whole nipple into her mouth and began to suck.

The mother's eyes flashed her gratitude and she said something in Greek, which Nicole did not understand.

'You've made a conquest there,' Dr Capodistrias said when they were outside the door. 'She thinks you should have babies of your own.'

'Oh, you mean at my advanced age,' Nicole quipped lightly.

'I don't see why you can't accept a compliment in the spirit in which it is given.' His voice was stern and superior.

'I'm sorry. I just don't think I'll have babies, that's all . . .'

'Everyone should have babies.' His solemn pronouncement took her by surprise. 'They are our investment for the future.'

'And have you made your own investment?' She could have bitten out her tongue as soon as she'd said it. It was his pontificating she objected to, but that was no excuse for being rude to the great man.

His eyes misted over for a moment, before he turned and moved away without answering. She must have hit on a sore point.

'Would you like to see your room, Sister?' Nurse Stangos asked hurriedly.

'My room? But I shall be living out.'

'Yes, of course, but you'll need a base here, and there'll be some nights when it won't be possible to get home.'

'And split duties, when you'll need a siesta.' Alexander Capodistrias turned back, and his firm, even voice gave nothing away. 'It gets very hot in the middle of summer. There'll be times when you'll be physically incapable of climbing back up the kali strata.' He smiled amiably. 'I'll show you to your room, and then I'll take you to dinner. I expect you're starving.'

'Yes, but I thought Nurse Stangos might need some help.'

'No, that's all right, Sister. We can manage,' Nurse Stangos assured her. 'I'll see you in the morning.'

'This way.' The doctor led, and Nicole followed him out through the end door, across a pebbled courtyard to a small, ancient, newly renovated villa. 'Staff quarters,' he announced, pushing open a heavy oak door. 'We've all got a room here. This is yours. It's not locked; as I told you earlier, we never lock anything.'

She walked into the cool room, with its pretty flowered curtains. There were coloured tapestries on the walls, and a large vase of flowers, predominantly roses and bougainvillaea, had been placed on a low table. It was small but adequate. A narrow bed with a patchwork quilt took up most of one wall, and there was a tiny shower room.

'How splendid! I hadn't expected such luxury.' Nicole looked around her admiringly.

'On such a backward island . . .' Alexander added.

'I didn't say that.' Her blue eyes flashed ominously.

'No, but you meant it. Come on, let's go for dinner. I haven't eaten a thing all day.'

She wanted to decline his invitation. He was only being polite to her, on her first day at work, and it was a terrible strain trying to be polite to him. She would have much preferred to kick off her sandals and lie down on the inviting bed for a well-earned rest. It wasn't as if he even liked her, and the feeling was mutual. She found him over-bearing and pompous, but yet, there was something electrifyingly attractive about him that pulled her, magnetically, towards him. If things had been different, she might easily have fallen for him . . . but that would have been ridiculous! You can't fall for someone you don't even like . . .

'Well, are you ready?' His impatient question brought Nicole back to earth. She realised she had been standing in the middle of the room, staring at the flowers.

'What lovely roses,' she murmured absently.

He reached forward, picking out one of the tiny flowers she hadn't seen, and held it towards her. 'Forget-me-not.' His tone was bantering but disturbing. 'The colour of your eyes, I think.' He moved closer to take a better look. His mouth was just above her face. She could imagine it lowering and touching hers. Hurriedly she stepped back before her fantasies got the better of her.

There was a look of surprise in Alexander's brilliant eyes, before he turned and made for the door. 'Let's go.'

The dark, velvet night had fallen when they stepped out on to the mosaic courtyard. A bright moon illuminated Ceres Bay, and myriads of tiny stars twinkled in the deep purple sky. The sound of laughter and Greek music played on a bouzoúki drifted up from one of the tavernas. It might be fun after all to dine out in Ceres with the eminent doctor.

'My father is expecting me home for dinner,' he said, abruptly, shattering her idea of a carefree taverna evening. 'He'd like to meet you.'

'And I'd like to meet him,' Nicole replied courteously, masking her disappointment.

They took the steps route down to the harbour, where Dominic was waiting for them in a shiny silver speed-boat. His face shone with happiness as Alexander Capodistrias approached along the quayside. He held out his hand to help Nicole aboard, before untying the ropes and starting the engine. As they sped away from the quayside, a thousand coloured lights formed an irridescent rainbow on the surface of the water, rippling in concentric circles.

The boat rounded the headland and sailed into Symborio Bay. The bright moonlight illuminated the outline of the hills, sweeping majestically down to the sea. As the boat approached the shore, Nicole could make out an imposing white building nestling at the foot of a hill above the sea. Its white, crenellated façade gave it the appearance of a small castle.

Alexander Capodistrias placed an arm casually on her shoulders. 'There's the house.' His deep, mellow voice so close to her had an unnerving effect, but it was the touch of his fingers that set her pulses racing. She remained absolutely still, not breathing, until he moved away to speak to Dominic.

They came in to land at a long wooden jetty. Dominic leapt out to tie up, and Nicole, not being used to boats, hesitated for a moment until the vessel had stopped completely. In a lightning movement she felt herself being scooped up from behind into strong arms, before being dumped unceremoniously on to the jetty. She landed on her feet, but turned furiously to look at the doctor. He evaded her eyes and shook his head at Dominic. 'Women! Such helpless creatures!' he said with an amused smile as he leapt off the boat.

Dominic grinned as he secured the boat firmly.

'This way, Sister,' the doctor said. 'Or may I call you Nicole?'

'If you wish,' she replied, coldly.

'And you may call me Alexander.'

She held her breath. That was something she was going to find very difficult. Following behind him on the narrow jetty, she tried to keep pace with his long strides. Steep steps took them to a wide-open door that led into a courtyard. It was very grand, with marble pillars and huge antique vases, discreetly illuminated by hidden lights.

They went through into the main house to where an elderly white-haired man was sitting on the balcony watching the sea. He turned and raised his hand in welcome.

'Alexander! I saw you coming over the water. I'd almost given you up for lost. Do introduce me to your friend.'

'This is Nicole Langley, Father; you know, our new nursing sister. Guess where I found her . . . At the surgery, this morning—or rather, she found me.'

His boyish exuberance removed the cold exterior of his polished personality, and Nicole could see what he must have been like before the cares and responsibilities of the medical profession changed him.

'My dear, I'm delighted to meet you. Sit down here beside me, and tell me all about yourself. It's so long since I was in England,' the old man said warmly.

'Father, we've both had a hard day. I'm going to ask Eirene to serve dinner,' Alexander cut in.

'Yes, of course, but relax for a few minutes first. Have a drink, my boy.' He gestured with his hand, and an old Greek servant came forward with a drinks tray and started to pour a colourless aperitif into glasses. 'When you have only one son, as I have, it's not surprising that I should want him to spend some time with his old father. Do you take water with your ouzo, my dear?'

'I don't know,' Nicole said hesitantly.

'I thought you'd been here for a week, already,' Alexander laughed. 'What a sheltered existence you must have had.' He poured some water into her drink and it turned cloudy. 'I think we'd better dilute it for you, in that case. *Yásoo!*' He raised his glass.

'What does that mean?' she asked curiously.

'Roughly translated it means good health, or cheers.'

'*Yásoo*,' she said shyly, and raised the glass to her lips.

'Wow!' For a moment she forgot the courteous manners she had adopted in this distinguished company.

Alexander smiled. 'It's strong stuff, isn't it?'

She swallowed hard and nodded. 'You could say that.' Turning to the older man, she asked, 'How are you now, after your coronary, Dr Capodistrias?'

'Oh, please call me Demetrius. Otherwise, I shall feel even older than my three score years and ten.' He grinned mischievously, and the old eyes twinkled. 'I'm feeling much better, thank you, my dear, although everyone insists I should rest.'

'I should think so, too.' Nicole was unable to keep the professional concern out of her voice. 'I must admit, I was amazed to see you sitting out here, sir—I mean Demetrius.'

'I'm a tough old bird. I guess they'll have to shoot me in the end.'

A plump, dark woman in a black dress, covered by a spotless white apron, appeared in the doorway smiling.

'Dinner's ready, Father.' Alexander stood up and offered his arm to Nicole with a ceremonial flourish.

'Shouldn't you help your father?' she asked, concerned about Demetrius.

'Don't worry about me,' said the old man, standing up easily. 'I can manage.'

And indeed he could! Nicole watched, full of admiration, as he walked to the table and sat down at the head. When Alexander steered her to her place, she was aware of the soft touch of his fingers under her arm. He can certainly be gallant when it suits him, she thought uncharitably. But she remembered the feel of his hand long after he had removed it.

Alexander reached across the table and helped Nicole to the first course, from a large serving dish. 'Dolmádes and tzatziki—that's stuffed vine leaves with yoghurt and garlic,' he explained.

She found the unusual combination of tastes very appetizing. The next course was kalamari, which turned out to be baby squid, followed by a main course of souvlakia, or kebabs, with green beans.

'Eirene would have made one of her special desserts if we'd known you were coming.' Demetrius sounded apologetic. 'As it is, there's only fruit and cheese.'

'That sounds delightful,' Nicole said with relief. It would be difficult to eat anything more after the first three courses.

The sound of muffled voices drifted through the open window as Eirene was serving the cheese. Alexander stood up and crossed restlessly out on to the balcony.

'They're here again, Father.' His voice was quiet, but the tone was urgent.

Demetrius pushed back his chair and hurried over to join his son.

'You shouldn't rush about like that . . .' Nicole began to remonstrate, but the old man was oblivious to her concern. Puzzled, she left the table and moved towards them.

Father and son were staring over the edge of the balcony at a vessel which had moored some way from their private landing stage. In the bright moonlight she could make out a large white luxury yacht, probably about thirty feet long. The sails were furled against the tall masts which pointed up towards the dark sky.

'Go back to the table, Nicole!' Alexander's peremptory command took her by surprise, but she turned automatically in response to the authoritarian tone.

'Alexander! Is that any way to speak to a guest?' Demetrius was incensed at his son's discourtesy.

'I'm sorry, Father, but I don't want anyone involved

until we know . . .' He broke off in mid-sentence, obviously sensing that he had said too much already.

Confused and dejected, Nicole returned to the table. Whatever it was he didn't want her to know, was no concern of hers. She was here as a nursing sister and that was all that mattered.

'Come, my dear; let's go into the drawing room for some coffee.' Demetrius' soothing tone helped to pacify her as he accompanied her into the next room. Alexander was still on the balcony and as far as Nicole was concerned, he could stay there! She sank down into the cushions of a velvet sofa, and accepted a tiny cup of thick black, Greek coffee.

It was a charming room, lavishly furnished, and enhanced by bold, crimson damask curtains, held back with golden silk tassels. In the centre of the room stood a well-polished mahogany grand piano.

'Do you play, Demetrius?' She stood up and walked across to admire the instrument.

'No, my dear; that was my wife's.' The old man joined her and pointed to a photograph in the centre of the piano. 'This was Charlotte,' he said lovingly, 'before she was taken from us.' There was a tremor of deep emotion in his voice, and a large tear trickled down his cheek.

'I'm sorry.' What else could she say? It was inadequate, but words could never ease the pain of bereavement.

There was another photograph beside Charlotte's. An attractive dark-haired woman was smiling down at a young boy, who bore a remarkable resemblance to her. Mother and son, obviously. 'Who's this?' she asked tentatively, hoping to take the old man's mind off his wife.

'That's my daughter-in-law, Vanessa, and my grandson Marcus.'

Her heart started pounding again. From somewhere in the background she could hear the shrilling of a telephone. She was trying to concentrate her thoughts as she remembered Demetrius' words earlier that evening, '*When you have only one son, as I do . . .*' So this daughter-in-law must be . . . Why was it that she felt a stab of resentment? It had nothing to do with her if Alexander had a wife and child.

'How old is your grandson?' she asked, to hide her confusion.

The old man sighed heavily. 'He, alas, is no longer with us. If he'd lived, he would have been about . . . let me see . . .'

'Father, we'll have to go.' Alexander's timely arrival spared Nicole any further embarrassment.

She felt she had opened up too many old wounds. It must have seemed so insensitive, and that was the last thing she wanted.

Alexander's urgent tone cut across her troubled thoughts. 'That was the hospital—there's been an accident. The two taxis have had a head-on collision on the water-front . . .'

Nicole's attention focused immediately on the emergency. 'Goodbye, Demetrius. Thank you for the dinner,' she addressed the old man, before following Alexander quickly out of the house and down to the jetty.

CHAPTER THREE

THE sleek silver boat glided effortlessly across the moon-lit water of Symborio Bay. Nicole glanced nervously in the direction of the mysterious yacht, brightly illumi-nated against the dark hillside. She could hear the sound of voices and laughter, and longed to ask questions, but one look at Alexander's stern, impassive face warned her not to. He was staring straight ahead and seemed to have lost all interest in the vessel in his haste to reach the car crash victims. Nicole, too, found herself worrying about what they would find when they reached hospital. She would have liked to have spent more time there before being plunged into an emergency situation.

Dominic, who had appeared immediately when Alexander had sent for him, steered the boat out of Symborio Bay towards Ceres harbour. The brilliant lights from the little town twinkled on the water, but the gay, carefree atmosphere had dwindled away in the wake of the first road accident on the island. Groups of disconsolate men gathered at the water's edge, peering out to watch the arrival of the great doctor who was going to make everything all right. Some of them had witnessed the awful crash, and were still shocked with disbelief. Things like this just didn't happen on Ceres—in the rest of the world, yes—but here! It was unthinkable . . .

'Are they going to be all right, Doctor?' was the question voiced by the islanders as Alexander and Nicole jumped ashore.

Alexander murmured soothing words to the anxious

onlookers. 'It's too early to say. We'll do what we can . . .'

They hurried up the steps to the hospital and went straight to the tiny Casualty Department. Staff Nurse Stangos raised her head with relief from the prostrate figure on the stretcher.

'Dr Capodistrias, thank goodness you've arrived!'

'Now, who have we got here?' The doctor's voice was calm and reassuring as he looked down at the young man.

'This is Sergio, Doctor. He was driving back from the upper town in his taxi—fortunately without a passenger —when he collided with the other taxi and went off the quay-side into the water. He managed to escape through the open window and swim to the surface.'

The wide-open eyes, staring up from the stretcher, conveyed their terror and bewilderment. The dark, curly hair hung in limp wisps over Sergio's unnaturally pale forehead. Alexander made a brief examination.

'He's in deep shock. Make him comfortable, keep him warm, give him fluids—you know the routine, Nurse Stangos. I'll see him again when I've attended to the other two patients.' He was already moving across to the remaining stretchers.

'This is Setiris, sir, the driver of the other taxi, and Yannis, his passenger. He's a waiter and was returning home to Epano, after work.' The staff nurse turned back to comfort Sergio, who had begun to sob quietly.

Setiris and Yannis were fully conscious and seemed in considerable pain.

'Fetch some Pethidine, Sister.' Alexander eased back the bloodstained sheet, to begin his examination. 'And bring me a white coat, Nurse Stangos—and one for Sister.' His eyes swept briefly over the chic white dress Nicole was wearing, and she found herself looking forward to putting on a uniform again. It would create a welcome barrier between them.

After several minutes he raised his head and smiled. 'Not as bad as I thought. Setiris has some fractured metatarsals. I'll check that with an X-ray, but I'm almost certain. It should be fairly simple to set the foot in plaster of Paris. Apparently, part of the engine came through on impact. And there's an obvious fracture of the clavicle . . .'

'Would you like me to put a figure-of-eight bandage on it?' Nicole was anticipating the surgeon's demands.

He glanced shrewdly at her. 'Is that what you would recommend, at the Benington, Sister?' His tone was dry, and his eyes humourless as he looked at her.

She knew he was mocking her, and it threw her completely. 'I'm sorry, sir.'

'Sorry? For what?' Alexander asked.

'I was trying to be helpful . . .'

'I'm the surgeon, you're the sister; perhaps you could remember that. In many cases it's not necessary to bind the clavicle.'

'But in this particular case, sir . . .' Nicole paused again, looking down at the distortion in the patient's collar-bone, but she was aware of the different schools of thought in orthopaedics and decided not to argue.

'As a matter of fact, I agree with you.' The warmth in his deep, mellow voice surprised Nicole. She felt he was simply trying to make a point, to keep her in her place. 'By all means, put your bandage on,' he conceded with a broad smile.

As she looked at the wide, sensuous mouth and the shining green-hazel eyes, she swallowed her pride. He could be such a beast! But she wasn't going to rise to his bait. She found herself wondering how his wife could stand such a male chauvinist; but perhaps he didn't try to humiliate her. Maybe he treated her gently and lovingly . . . Deliberately she brought her thoughts back to the patient.

'I'll give the Pethidine, now, sir,' Nicole said.

'By all means. Then do the bandage and clean the blood from his face. We'll have to put a couple of stitches in that chin.'

Alexander started to examine the next patient, Yannis. After a few minutes, Dominic wheeled in the X-ray machine and it was found that the young waiter had a fractured scaphoid bone in the wrist.

'Bring some plaster of Paris and all the apparatus, Dominic. We'll work in here.'

Nicole found she couldn't help admiring the ease with which the surgeon switched from one task to another. He was certainly adaptable, having to perform in a variety of capacities, which would be unheard of in a large hospital. She had never assisted in the application of plaster of Paris, and she was grateful for his explicit instructions as she plunged one of the special bandages into water.

'Hold it there until the air bubbles have stopped rising. Okay. Lift it out and compress it, gently, towards the centre . . . that's fine . . . hand it to me . . . now put the next one in water while I'm rolling this one on.'

It was not an easy task, and when it was finished and the fractures had been immobilised in plaster, she felt greatly relieved. She looked across at the exacting surgeon and found that he, too, had relaxed and lost some of his previous tension.

'Thank you, Sister. You could always get a job as an orthopaedic technician, if you get tired of nursing.'

She resented his patronising tone. 'I shall never tire of nursing. I love my work,' she said quietly.

'I can see that.'

Was he, at last, paying her a compliment? She raised her eyes to his, and found herself confused by the expression on his face. Hurriedly, she looked away. 'I'd like to settle the patients in their beds, Doctor. Perhaps Dominic could . . .'

'Dominic will take one trolley; I'll take the other.' He sounded brisk.

Now he was going to act as hospital porter! She suppressed a smile as she watched the eminent surgeon pushing his trolley down the corridor. The staff of St Celine's would have been amazed to see him!

Staff Nurse Stangos had already settled Sergio into a bed, and prepared two others in the same room. Nicole fixed an orthopaedic cradle over Setiris' leg, leaving the end of the covers open to dry the plaster. She checked temperature, pulse and respiration, acutely aware that the surgeon was watching her.

What's he waiting for? He's written up the drugs, and the patients are almost asleep . . .

'Come along to the common room when you've finished, Sister,' he said curtly.

It sounded like an order, so her reaction was automatic. 'Yes, sir.' She heard him go out and close the door, but did not look up from her task.

After a few minutes, a young Greek night nurse came in and stood beside her. 'Shall I take over from you, Sister?' she asked.

'Thank you. I've almost finished,' Nicole replied. 'Stay with the orthopaedic patients, and make constant checks on their circulation. Report to me if you're worried. I'll be in the common room for the next few minutes.'

She paused by Sergio's bedside on her way out, and was pleased to see that he was breathing easily. She reached over and found his pulse had returned to normal. As she took her fingers away, he opened his eyes and smiled.

'*Efharistó*—thank you, Sister,' he murmured softly.

'Go back to sleep,' she whispered, tucking the covers around his shoulders. As she turned away, she thought about what would have happened if the young taxi driver had not escaped through the car window, or if he had been unable to swim. She shuddered involuntarily, and went out into the corridor.

Dr Capodistrias was waiting for her in the common room. He placed a small glass in front of her. 'Drink that,' he ordered.

'What is it?' Nicole asked.

'Metaxa—it's a Greek brandy. You look tired; it will revive you.'

She raised the glass to her lips and gasped as the smooth golden liquid scorched the back of her throat.

He laughed at her reaction. 'I only recommend it for medicinal use, and then only in small quantities. How do you feel?'

'Better.' She sank into a comfortable armchair and faced him with a nervous smile. 'What did you want to see me about?'

'Purely social reasons. To finish off our evening, which was interrupted.' He gave her a strange smile, and she felt an unaccustomed tingling in her toes. His smile was enough to melt the hardest heart. However she tried to dislike this man, he had a way of captivating her again with a single look.

'I thought your father looked remarkably well, considering his recent heart attack,' Nicole began in a polite, sociable voice.

'You are an expert on cardiology, then?' His eyes were dazzlingly dangerous as he looked at her.

'Of course not.' Oh, why did he have to spoil the

pleasant atmosphere? 'I've worked with cardiac patients, and I feel that my training . . .'

'Exactly,' Alexander interrupted her. 'Your training has made you into a professional, so therefore you should know better than to make idle remarks about the state of my father's health. Without a thorough examination, you cannot possibly . . .'

'I merely said your father looked well, in view of the fact that he'd had a coronary,' Nicole retorted. It was impossible to keep the exasperation from her voice. He was the one who had sent for her to finish off their social evening, but he seemed to have no idea how to bridge the gap that was widening between them.

She stood up and walked across to the balcony, deliberately keeping her back towards him. 'Perhaps I should have made a remark about the weather, instead.' She looked out across the dark waters of the harbour. 'I don't think you could take exception to that.'

He was on his feet and crossing the room. She knew he was standing directly behind her because she could feel his breath fanning the back of her neck. Motionless, she watched the pink glow behind the mountain peak across the bay.

'It's almost dawn. The sun's rising.' The closeness of his deep voice sent shivers down her spine. At least they were on neutral ground now; the sunrise had nothing to do with medicine.

She dared to turn round and raise her eyes to his. 'I hadn't realised we'd been here so long.'

He smiled. 'You're so dedicated to your work, aren't you?' With a long, sensitive finger he tilted her chin upwards. 'Did anyone ever tell you, you have the most beautiful blue eyes?'

She stared up at him and gave a little embarrassed laugh. 'Now you're making fun of me again. You sound like a character from a romantic film.'

'Do I? Well, it is rather romantic, standing here watching the sunrise.' The dazzling green-hazel eyes flickered briefly and she wondered if she had hurt him. Beneath that cold exterior there might be a warm, romantic element. He probably kept it hidden most of the time, from everyone except his wife.

She turned her back on him and watched the warm glow expanding over the hillside. The rosy pink colour behind the peak was changing to a vivid crimson.

'You mustn't stare at the sunrise for too long. It will hurt your eyes,' Alexander said softly.

He placed his hands lightly on her shoulders and she revelled in the nearness of that broad, manly chest. He had removed his white coat, and she could feel the warmth of his skin through the thin cotton shirt. There was a faint, tantalising aroma of expensive aftershave. They watched in silence as the huge round ball of fire rose from behind the mountain. Nicole had never seen the sun rise before and it was a primeval experience for her. She felt like Eve, in the garden of Eden with Adam, at the dawn of the world . . .

'Dr Capodistrias, I'd like a word with you.'

The dream world was shattered by a cold female voice from across the other side of the room. Nicole turned abruptly, her short fair hair brushing against Alexander's shoulder. A small thin, angular lady wearing a black dress with a white apron, was standing in the doorway. From the set of her bony shoulders to the firm stance of the flat black lace-up shoes, she conveyed her disapproval.

'I have just come from the newly admitted patients . . .'

'Sister Croney, I don't think you've met our new Sister-in-Charge. This is Sister Langley.' Alexander was in control of the situation, as he faced the irate figure.

'That's what I came to see you about, Doctor.' Sister Croney swept into the room like a hurricane, the large white cap bobbing dangerously on the crimpy grey waves. 'I've just come from the new patients, and I was informed by one of my night nurses—*my* night nurses . . .'

She paused for effect, but Alexander merely gave a sigh of resignation, so she continued in the same harsh tone, the clipped Greek accent becoming more and more pronounced with her growing agitation.

'My night nurse informed me that the new sister had told her to report to *her*.'

There was a lull in the storm as she pursed her lips and glared at the doctor.

'Sister Croney, I merely asked the nurse to let me know if she was worried about her patients,' Nicole put in quietly.

'But I'm in charge at night, Sister Langley.' The grey head trembled angrily.

'That's not exactly true.' Alexander's voice was firm. 'Sister Langley has been appointed to take charge of the hospital as a whole, so if she is here, then naturally . . .'

'Oh, I know what you all think of me, but where would this hospital be if I didn't come here every night—night after night?'

The older woman looked close to tears, and Nicole stepped towards her. 'I'm sure we're all very grateful for your work, Sister. It's a pity we have to start off like this.'

She had no idea who this woman was. Why was she wearing a black uniform? Nicole was sure that her own Sister's uniform was dark blue. Maybe she wore black because it was night-time. Unexpectedly, the thought made her want to giggle, but she kept a straight face as she held out a conciliatory hand.

'I'm sure we'll be able to sort out our working relationship, Sister. It's early days, and changes in routine are always difficult. Let's shake on it and start again.'

Sister Croney hesitated, and then reluctantly put out her arm and allowed Nicole to shake her hand. It was cold and clammy, and Nicole kept the encounter brief.

'I'm glad you're here, because I'm dead beat. I'd like to go and get some sleep before the morning work. I was only saying to Dr Capodistrias a moment ago that I hadn't realised how late it was.'

'Or early, whichever way you like to look at it.' There was no doubt about the admiration in the surgeon's eyes as he looked down at Nicole.

'Well, I must get back to my work.' The night sister walked briskly towards the door.

'Yes, you do that. I'll be along in a minute.' Alexander's eyes stayed on Nicole as the older woman swept out.

'My, my; quite the little diplomat, aren't you?' he said softly. 'I like the way you handled her.'

'Who is she?'

'We inherited her with the pharmacy, I'm afraid,' Alexander told her. 'When my father first became a doctor on the island, she was the self-appointed authority on all medical matters. He had to keep her on, although she's totally without qualifications. She means well, but it's a terrible strain. Some of her ideas are so archaic!'

'She must be very old if she was here when your father started,' Nicole was incredulous.

'Medicine is his second career. He had a fleet of ships until he was thirty-four. Then he became disillusioned with his jet-set life, so he sold all his shipping interests and trained as a doctor. When he qualified, he came back to Ceres and devoted himself to the islanders.' Alexander's voice showed the pride he felt for his father.

'So he must have been about forty when he started here?' Nicole was impressed by what she had heard.

'Something like that. And Sister Croney was probably in her late twenties. She was always trying to flirt with my father, apparently.' He grinned boyishly, displaying pearly teeth in the wide, sensuous mouth.

Nicole took a deep breath to check her fluttering heart. 'I expect he was very handsome in those days.' Just like you . . . He would gaze into the eyes of his young nurse, as you are doing now. And, like you, he was already married to someone else, so nothing came of it. Sister Croney buried herself in her work and became an embittered old maid . . .

'What's the matter, Nicole?' His shrewd eyes searched her face.

She gave a start as she brought her thoughts back to the present. 'Nothing; I'm tired, that's all. I'll go and get some rest, if you don't need me.'

'You mustn't come on duty until after midday—and that's an order, young lady. I presume you're going to stay in your room, here?'

She nodded, suddenly feeling deflated and utterly exhausted. She wanted to escape from those searching eyes to the safety of her little room. He had no right to look at her like that. She hurried out into the corridor.

There was no sign of life as she reached the staff quarters and crossed the mosaic courtyard. She pushed open the door to her room. The smell of flowers was heavy in the air. On the low table she could see the vase, but the forget-me-not Alexander had picked out for her was lying on the floor, where she had dropped it. She picked it up and stared at it for a moment. It would be a pity to put it back with the other bigger flowers. They would eclipse its frail beauty.

She reached for one of the books on the narrow shelf and pressed the forget-me-not between the pages, telling herself she would start a collection of the island flowers. Then she climbed quickly into the little bed and closed her heavy lids.

It was a long time before she fell asleep. The events of the last twenty-four hours kept flooding back to disturb her. And Alexander was always there; even when she fell asleep, he was in her dreams, staring at her with a hauntingly enigmatic expression.

CHAPTER FOUR

THE sun was streaming into her room when she opened her eyes. With a start, she realised she was not alone. A young girl dressed in a brightly coloured dress was sweeping the tiled floor, humming quietly to herself as she did so. That must have been what had awoken her. She sat up in bed and the maid turned and smiled.

'*Kaliméra.*'

'*Kaliméra*—good morning,' Nicole replied.

Encouraged by Nicole's attempt at the Greek language, the girl launched into a rapid, friendly discourse which was quite incomprehensible.

Nicole laughed and shook her head. '*Borite na millissete pio arghá sas parakaló . . .* Please speak slowly.'

'*Daxi*—okay.' The maid grinned at Nicole, displaying strong white teeth in the dark, olive skinned face. She started again, this time much slower, and Nicole was able to grasp the overall message. The girl was apologising for waking her up. Slowly and carefully, Nicole replied that it did not matter. She wanted to get up anyway.

'*Posseleni?* What's your name?' Nicole asked.

'Taxiahoula.' The maid was now leaning on her broom, prepared for a long conversation.

'Taxiahoula; what a lovely name. I'm going to have a shower.'

The girl nodded and produced a towel and soap. Nicole took them gratefully. She would have to bring some of her own things down here from the studio in Epano. It looked as if she was going to spend more time

46

than she had thought here at the hospital. She padded across the cool tiles in her bare feet, in to the shower.

When she emerged, refreshed, Taxiahoula had laid out her uniform on the bed. It consisted of a dark blue cotton dress, with a fluffy lace cap. The maid was waiting to help her dress, although Nicole would have preferred to try it on by herself. When at last she stood in front of the long mirror, the maid clapped her hands in delight. Nicole liked the well-cut dress with its broad belt, but she wasn't sure about the cap. It was too fluffy and frivolous—made her look like a bride! She wondered who had designed it. Certainly not poor old Sister Croney—her own cap had been more like a flour bag!

Nicole wandered out into the courtyard.

The maid called something after her, and she caught the word *'proghevma'*—breakfast.

'Oh, yes please—*né, parakaló*.'

Taxiahoula told her to sit down and wait; she would bring it along.

There were several small tables in the sun-dappled courtyard, their shiny white paint reflecting the bright morning light. A young man in a white coat was sitting over in the corner under an olive tree.

'Why don't you join me, Sister? I've got the only table in the shade,' he called in a friendly voice.

'Thank you.' She crossed the uneven stones, the sun already hot on her head, and sat down at the shady table.

'Let me introduce myself; I'm Nikos Seferis.' He held out his hand.

'Nicole Langley. Have you been at the hospital long, Dr Seferis?'

'Oh, please call me Nick,' he grinned amiably. 'I've only just qualified, and I can't get used to the new title. This is my first job and I'm a new arrival.'

'That makes two of us.' Nicole liked this friendly

young Greek. There was a freshness in the way he smiled
that was very welcoming.

'Your English is very good,' she said.

Nikos grinned. 'I've spent several years in England.'

'That's useful; my Greek is still basic, so I might have
to use you as an interpreter.'

'Feel free.' He gave her an encouraging smile that lit
up the whole of his sun-tanned face.

Nicole found herself admiring his strong physique. He
looked like a man who enjoyed body-building and out-
door sports. The powerful muscles bulged through the
sleeves of his white coat, giving him a massive appearance, although Nicole doubted if he were more than
medium height.

Taxiahoula arrived and placed bread rolls, coffee, a
dish of peach jam and soft butter on the table.

'*Efharistó*,' Nicole said.

'Ah, so you *do* speak the language.' Nikos was
watching her with amusement.

'I'm brilliant on please and thank you, but beyond that
it's something of a strain,' she told him.

As they both laughed, a shadow fell across the table.

'Dr Seferis—I was hoping to find you in the hospital
by now.' Alexander Capodistrias eased his long frame
into a chair beside Nicole.

'I'm sorry, sir. I had to unpack my things after I got off
the morning boat . . .' Nikos began.

'And chat up my new Sister, and drink coffee and so
on. All perfectly understandable on your first day, I
suppose.' The surgeon's voice was dangerously languid.
'You'll soon find that we expect very high standards
here. In fact, my code of ethics is the same as it is at St
Celine's. This is not some uncivilised hospital, even if it
is situated on a somewhat undeveloped island.'

Nicole was loath to interfere, but she felt that Alexander was being grossly unfair to the new member of staff. She glanced at the stern, aristocratic features. Was this really the man who had stood behind her, watching the sunrise, earlier today?

'I hope you are rested, Sister,' Alexander turned to Nicole.

'Yes, thank you, sir.'

'Good. Then perhaps we can get on with some work. I know I told you to come in late, but we're rather busy, so if you would like to . . .'

'Do you mind if I finish my breakfast first?' Nicole asked, but the hint of sarcasm appeared lost on the eminent doctor.

'Not at all. I'll have a coffee with you.' He waved a hand towards the maid. *'Éna kafe, parakaló.'*

Taxiahoula dropped her duster on the floor and ran to the kitchen, a happy smile on her face. She adored Dr Capodistrias. His father had brought her into the world and her family worshipped him. She returned and placed the tiny cup of Greek coffee in front of Alexander, waiting for some sign that he recognised her.

'Taxiahoula.' He was asking something about her mother, but speaking too quickly for Nicole to understand. She watched the young girl's face shining with pleasure.

He seemed to enjoy a kind of hero worship on the island. He basked in the reflected glory of his philanthropic father, and he had only to lift his finger and the islanders came running! No wonder he's conceited, pompous, arrogant. She wasn't going to fall into the same trap . . . oh no! Deliberately, she took her time over her breakfast, aware that he had already finished his coffee. Then she began to think about the patients; perhaps they were really busy in the hospital. She drained her coffee and stood up.

'I'm ready, now, Doctor.'

He jumped to his feet, and Nick Seferis almost upset the table in his anxiety to be first to open the door for the great man.

'Crawler!' whispered Nicole, and the young doctor smiled sheepishly.

'It can't do any harm,' he muttered as they hurried behind the tall, irascible figure.

A harassed Staff Nurse Stangos raised her head from the reception hall desk and smiled with relief. She had been trying to cope with junior staff, and the sight of the new Sister and Doctor was most welcome.

'Is it convenient to do a round now, Staff?' Dr Capodistrias was at his most polite when dealing with Nurse Stangos. She was an excellent nurse but she lacked confidence.

'Certainly, sir.' She came round the desk and eyed the new doctor warily.

'This is Dr Seferis; Staff Nurse Stangos.'

They shook hands as Alexander watched with a benign smile.

'Dr Seferis is something of a celebrity at his own hospital in Athens. He carried off a few prizes during his training; am I right, Doctor?'

'Well, yes, sir. I see you've been checking up on me . . .' Nikos answered.

'I have, indeed.' The consultant's eyes were hard. 'I also found that you have no difficulty in passing exams, but you find practical work something of a bore . . .'

'Now, look here, sir . . .'

'No, you look here,' Alexander said sternly. 'This is not some idyllic Greek island where you can spend your time swanning around as you please. You are here to work—hard. If not, you might as well pack your bags and go straight back to Athens.'

The young doctor's face remained impassive, but a thin trickle of sweat appeared on his forehead. Alexander had finally got through to him. Nicole watched the two men with bated breath. It was a contest of wits. She knew very well that Alexander was testing him—just as he had tested her—but she wondered if Nick knew what was going on.

'I know the score, sir,' he said quietly.

'Good.' Capodistrias smiled, as if he had just delivered a speech of welcome. 'Let's start with the new patients. Perhaps you would lead the way, Sister . . .'

Nicole gathered her thoughts and set off briskly down the corridor, terribly aware of the tension behind her. She pushed open a door and went into the new patients' room.

Sergio was sitting up in bed, listening to the radio with his earphones. He pulled them off and smiled at Nicole.

'Thanks for looking after me last night, Sister. You were great.'

Nicole smiled back. 'You were pretty good yourself. How are you feeling?'

'Much better, but my chest's still sore.'

'Let's have a look, shall we? Mm . . .' Nicole had opened the young man's shirt, and Alexander stepped forward with his stethoscope at the ready.

The chest was extensively scarred and bruised from his underwater battle with the car door, and the subsequent attempts at resuscitation. The surgeon ran expert fingers lightly over the skin. Sergio winced.

'There's a fractured rib here, Sergio . . . no, don't look so worried. It's not serious. We don't even need to bind it up. The other ribs will support it until it heals —that is, unless Sister prefers to put a bandage on . . .'

'No, I agree with you, sir,' Nicole said quietly.

A flicker of a smile played on the consultant's lips.

'Well, that's something. It will take time to heal, Sergio,' he continued, in a kindly voice.

'But when can I go home, Doctor? My wife . . .'

'Ah, yes; I remember, you were married recently, weren't you?' Everyone on Ceres knew when there was a wedding, and Alexander had heard about this one soon after he arrived.

'Last week, sir.' His voice rose with the anguish of separation.

'Perhaps tomorrow, if you behave yourself, but take it easy when you get home—nothing violent!' Alexander told him.

The young taxi driver laughed, and grimaced immediately afterwards with the pain in his ribs. 'And what about driving, Doctor? I've got my living to make.'

'I'm sure Setiris will be happy to look after your clients, won't you, Setiris?' Alexander perched himself easily on the next bed.

'That's what I'm afraid of,' Sergio called after him.

'I'll be in here longer than you, I think,' said Setiris, as he looked down at the thick plaster on his leg.

'Not much longer.' Alexander held the X-rays up to the light. 'Clean breaks on four metatarsals; clavicle . . . just a question of time really, Setiris. Are you patient?'

'Not when I have to keep a family. Who's going to feed them if I can't work?' He shifted uneasily in his bed.

'Don't worry—we'll sort something out for you,' Alexander assured the young man.

Nicole glanced at the surgeon's unworried face. It was easy enough for him to make vague promises. She wondered if there was any sort of welfare system here. The high-and-mighty Capodistrias probably didn't deign to look into that kind of problem. It would be beneath him. She pulled the covers back from the bed cradle to expose the injured limb.

'Move your toes for me, Setiris,' she asked gently. 'Mm, that's good, don't you think?' She raised her head and looked across the plaster of Paris.

Alexander smiled at her, a warm, conspiratorial smile that sent the blood rushing to her face. The green-hazel eyes held hers, as if there was no-one else in the room, as if they were still watching the sunrise together . . .

Almost immediately the smile vanished. 'Sister is fond of imposing her opinions on me, Dr Seferis. Sometimes I have to disagree with her—not always—just occasionally.'

The consultant placed his long fingers on the patient's toes. 'How does that feel, Setiris? Any pain?'

'No, that's okay.' The patient looked more relaxed, as Nicole plumped up his pillows and poured him a drink of water.

Dr Seferis had been studying the notes carefully, but had barely looked at the patient. Alexander glanced at him.

'You're very quiet, Doctor. May we have the benefit of your learned opinion on this case?'

'Certainly, sir. For a start, I think there's too much plaster on this foot. I'm surprised we haven't got advanced cyanosis. I think we should cut back the plaster by at least an inch. After all, it's the metatarsals, not the phalanges, which are affected.'

Nicole drew in a sharp breath and waited. The surgeon's eyes narrowed ominously as he regarded the junior doctor.

'But there is no cyanosis; the toes are in excellent condition . . .' he said.

'I think you've been lucky, sir,' answered Nikos.

Nicole stepped between the two of them. 'Supposing we cut it back half an inch?' she said quickly.

A slow smile spread across the consultant's face. 'Our

diplomatic Sister is proposing a compromise. Shall we agree with her, Seferis?'

The young doctor grinned, and the tension eased. 'Yes, sir.'

'And what do you think, Setiris?' Nicole smiled at the bewildered patient. 'Would you like me to cut back your plaster a little?'

'I don't care what you do, Sister, as long as you get me out soon, and back behind the wheel of my taxi.'

'We'll do what we can. You're in good hands,' she reassured him. 'Let me have a look at your collar bone . . . good. The displacement is less pronounced now.' She raised her eyes to look at Alexander.

'Yes; you were quite right to put that bandage on,' he told her. He traced the line of the fracture with expert fingers and smiled, before moving on to the next patient.

Yannis, the young waiter, was sitting beside his bed, resting his plastered arm on a pillow. 'Can I go home, Doctor?' he asked eagerly.

'Another one trying to escape from us! Is it so terrible in here?' Alexander's eyes were bright with amusement as he examined the fingers protruding from the plaster of Paris. 'I suppose you'd like to cut this back, Dr Seferis?'

'No, sir; I think you've got that one exactly right.'

'Do you? I'm so glad.' His sarcastic tone changed as he looked at the patient. 'How does it feel, Yannis?'

'Fine. It doesn't hurt at all.'

'Okay. You've convinced me.' The consultant smiled broadly as he dropped his professional manner. 'How's that delightful young sister of yours? The one that used to be such a pest when you came to play with Dominic . . .'

'She's seventeen—getting married soon,' Yannis replied proudly.

'No! I don't believe it. When's the wedding?'

'Next month. Will you come, Alexander? My mother would be delighted,' Yannis asked eagerly.

'I'll try. Send me an invitation.'

Nicole watched the easy relationship between them. She had noticed the way the young waiter had called the surgeon Alexander. That must stem from the days when he lived on the island and took an interest in its people. So, deep down, he had some of his father's philanthropic spirit, but she could never imagine him sacrificing his brilliant career to stay permanently on Ceres. He was much harder than his father.

'Perhaps you'd like to cut back Setiris' plaster now, Sister. Staff Nurse can finish the round with us. She knows the patients better than you, anyway.'

Capodistrias made his exit, with Nurse Stangos and Dr Seferis following in his wake. The young doctor turned in the doorway and gave Nicole a big wink. She smiled, and turned back to her patients.

'He's taken a fancy to you, Sister,' Yannis teased.

'Who?' she asked sharply.

'That young doctor. Who else?' The patient grinned at her confusion.

'Don't be silly,' she laughed. 'Now, are you ready to go, Yannis?' She put on her brisk Sister's manner.

He leapt to his feet. 'You bet. Staff Nurse told me when to come back to see Dr Capodistrias. He's a fantastic man, don't you think, Sister?'

'He seems to know his work . . .' Nicole hedged.

'Oh, come on. Who else would come flying out to help his sick father like that? He's very important in London . . .'

'I know,' she said dryly. 'Right; here's your bag. Can you manage it with the other hand? Will there be someone at home to look after you?'

'Of course.' Yannis seemed surprised at the question.

There was always at least one woman in the house; his mother, or his grandmother, or one of his sisters. He was looking forward to going home and being spoilt again. It was a good life for a man on Ceres. 'Goodbye, Sister; and thanks for everything.'

'Goodbye, Yannis.' She held the door open for the young man, before turning her attention to Setiris.

He looked vaguely uneasy when she produced a pair of plaster scissors, but she was quick to reassure him.

'Don't look so worried, Setiris.' She moved the bed cradle and leaned over the plaster. 'You won't feel a thing.'

As she began paring some of the excess plaster she kept an eye on the patient's face, to see how he was taking it. He seemed to have relaxed after the first few seconds.

'There—that was all right, wasn't it?' She straightened her back and put the scissors down on her tray.

'Have I still got all my toes?' he joked.

'I'll count them when I have a minute to spare. How many did you have?' Nicole quipped back.

The other taxi driver had been watching the proceedings almost enviously. He was bored with his inactivity and longing to get home to his young bride.

'Don't spend all your time with him, Sister. Come over here. I want you to look at my chest.'

'I've already looked at your chest, Sergio . . .'

'Well . . .' He grinned as he searched for another excuse for some attention. 'Don't you think you should put a bandage on it?'

'We've been into that already. Just lie still, and you'll soon be well enough to go home.' She smoothed his pillows and eased him back on to them.

'If only I wasn't a married man,' he said, amorously reaching out to touch her hair.

She ducked quickly and his hand knocked her frilly cap sideways. 'The sooner we get you back to your wife the better.'

He laughed as he watched her attempt to fix the cap back in place.

'All right, gentlemen; the cabaret's over. Try to behave yourself while I'm away.' She shook her head and smiled as she made a hasty retreat.

Out in the corridor, she secured the cap as best she could without the aid of a mirror. She would see to it later. Her main aim was to catch up with the round of the patients. It was true that Nurse Stangos knew them better than she did. Dr Capodistrias was right to point that out, but she would never get to know them unless she was given the chance to see them all.

She opened the door to the obstetrics room and spent some time helping with feeds. The young nurse welcomed an extra pair of hands and it was difficult to get away. The dear little newborn baby from yesterday had opened her eyes, and Nicole found herself drooling over her, almost as besotted as the mother.

'Who's a darling little girl, then? Who's beautiful . . . ?' she crooned.

She hadn't heard the door open, and the deep voice startled her.

'Charming; absolutely charming.' Dr Capodistrias surveyed the scene from the doorway. 'I thought you said you didn't like babies, Sister.'

'I adore them—other people's babies.' She handed the tiny bundle back to the mother.

'You sound like the poor old nanny in the song; "other people's babies, that's my lot . . ."'

Nicole laughed at his attempt to sing the tune, and as she caught the look in his eyes, she again wondered if she'd hurt his feelings.

'Do you think you could tear yourself away long enough to give me some help with a difficult patient?' Alexander's voice hardened slightly. 'I realise you would prefer to play around here all day, but we can't leave all the work to Nurse Stangos . . .'

'Of course. In actual fact, I'd hoped to catch you at the end of your round.' She moved towards the door.

'Not much chance of that if you waste your time . . .'

'I was *not* wasting time.' She lowered her voice, so as not to alarm the patients, and swept out into the corridor. He's *so* infuriating, this man! Without realising it, she clenched her fists tightly by her sides in frustration.

'Hey, don't get so mad.' He was standing beside her, looking down in what seemed like an approximation of concern. 'I have to crack the whip occasionally to keep everyone on their toes.'

You certainly do that, you slave-driver, she was thinking, but she smiled sweetly, and swallowed hard. He reached down and took hold of one of her tightly curled fists.

'We can't have this.' His voice was soft and gentle, as if he were talking to a child.

The touch of his hand on hers was electric. She felt him opening her fingers, smoothing the palm with his own, and then, in a sudden quick movement, he bent his head and brushed his lips lightly across the skin.

'That's better,' he murmured, almost to himself.

She gave an involuntary shiver. It was a kiss-and-make-up situation. He must have had plenty of practice, with his wife and child, because he did it expertly, and it didn't seem to affect him in the slightest. Whereas she found herself quivering with emotion. The palm of her hand was on fire . . .

She pulled it away, not daring to meet those brilliant,

searching eyes. If he noticed her distress, he made no indication as he moved off down the corridor.

'Nurse Stangos is holding the fort until we arrive. As I said, it's a difficult case.' His voice was coolly professional as Nicole hurried after him, trying to keep pace with his long strides. 'I've known Stavros since he was a boy—he's only eighteen . . .'

He pushed open the door of a room at the end of the corridor. In spite of her training, Nicole gasped at what she saw. A thin, emaciated figure was crouched on the floor, moaning quietly to himself, while Nurse Stangos bent over him making soothing noises. She looked across at them with relief.

'There was nothing I could do, Dr Capodistrias. He's just been sick again and . . .'

'That's all right, Ariadne. Thank you for looking after him. Sister can take over now.' He moved towards the crumpled figure, and the Staff Nurse went thankfully out of the door.

'Stavros, it's me, Alexander,' the surgeon said quietly.

At the sound of his voice, the patient lifted his head and reached out a bony arm. Nicole could see the watery eyes, the running nose, the shivering . . .

She had made her own diagnosis, even before she heard the fateful words.

'*Please*, Doctor. Give me some more. I just need one more fix and then I'll stop—you know I will. Just *one*! I feel as if I'm dying.'

Tears ran down the young man's face as he pleaded with the doctor. He bent his legs up to his chest, as if in agony.

'Abdominal cramps,' Nicole breathed, almost in disbelief. The diagnosis was classic. He had all the signs and symptoms. 'What are you going to do?' Her voice was harsher than she meant it to be, but for once in her nursing career she felt lost. She had no experience of drug addicts. Oh, yes, she'd read all the textbook jargon, but in England there were special treatment centres for patients like this. And she had never dreamed she would meet one here on this idyllic island.

She stared at Alexander as he soothed the demented boy. 'What are you going to do?' she repeated, almost hysterically.

'I'm going to give him some more.' His voice was quiet yet firm.

'You're *what*? Don't you realise the dangers . . .'

'I realise the dangers if I don't. If he's given a controlled dosage—less and less each time—we can obviate the withdrawal symptoms, and there's a possibility, only a possibility, that we can save him.'

She knew better than to argue with a doctor in front of a patient, but all her instincts rebelled against it. She wanted no part of this treatment, and yet she knew she had to agree to go along with it.

'In my room you'll find a small cupboard.' Alexander was holding out a key. 'I want you to go along and bring me . . .'

'No!' Her voice sounded distant and strange, even to her own ears. 'I'll stay with Stavros while you fetch the . . . whatever it is you've decided to give him.'

It was open rebellion, but she didn't care. He might be a distinguished consultant, but she didn't approve of his treatment in this particular case.

'Very well,' he said icily, and then, with more warmth, 'I won't be long, Stavros. Sister will look after you.'

Nicole moved towards the patient without glancing at Alexander. As the door closed, she placed her hands on the violently trembling shoulders, trying to calm away some of the young man's terror. It seemed an eternity before his return. Without looking up, she rolled up the tattered sleeve, wincing as she saw the scars on Stavros' arm.

With great difficulty, Alexander found a vein that was not already collapsed and gave his injection. Recovery was almost instantaneous. The patient stopped shivering and raised his head.

'Oh, thank you, Alexander. You're so kind. I won't trouble you again. You've saved my life. And you, Sister; I'm sorry if I caused you to worry.' He stood up.

'Wait a minute, Stavros. When did you last have something to eat?' Alexander faced his young patient, barring the way to the door.

A vague expression crossed the young man's face. 'Oh, I don't know—yesterday, perhaps.'

'Then you must stay and have some food—no, I insist.'

Stavros gave a sigh of resignation and sank down into an armchair. 'If you say so, sir.'

'I do. Sister, run along to the kitchen and see what you can find.' Alexander ordered. 'Wait here, Stavros; Sister will bring you a tray. I keep telling you, you *must* eat, if we're to get you better.'

'Okay, you're the boss.' The young man gave a grin, which made him look almost normal.

He must have been quite a good-looking boy before he became hooked on drugs, Nicole thought as she went out into the corridor. Alexander followed her, until they were out of earshot.

'Thanks for your help,' he said then. He sounded relieved.

She eyed him coldly. 'There was nothing else I could do, under the circumstances. I'll go and get his food.'

'No, wait, Nicole.' He put a hand on her arm.

'Yes?' She tried to sound calm.

'You may not approve of my methods, but in this particular case I know I'm right.' He was glaring down at her, willing her to contradict him.

'And what about psychotherapy?' she asked quietly.

'Yes, I agree, that's our ultimate aim. But we have to get the patient to a point at which he is willing to be helped. Very soon I hope to be able to treat him in this way.'

'So, meanwhile, we go along with his addiction?' Her blue eyes flashed ominously.

'A controlled dosage—giving him less and less each time,' Alexander explained.

'What's he on?'

'Heroin,' he answered in a calm, professional voice.

Nicole shivered. 'I'll go and get him something to eat.' Her eyes were wet with tears as she walked away. What a waste of a young life! How had he started? And why? And where was he getting the stuff from?

She pushed open the swing doors and went into the kitchen. A plump, amiable, round-faced cook looked up from her cooking pots and smiled at the new Sister.

'*Kaliméra,*' Nicole began, searching for the words she needed to produce some nourishing food for her patient. She walked over to the stove and looked into the iron pans. There was a delicious aroma of fresh vegetable soup, which the cook was preparing for lunch. That would be excellent, along with an omelette. It had to be a fairly light diet, if Stavros had not eaten for a while.

The cook launched into a voluble explanation of the mysteries of her cuisine. She liked the look of this new Sister; a bit on the skinny side, but she'd soon fatten her up. And she seems genuinely interested in my cooking, she thought, which makes a change. Pity, her Greek is so poor . . . we could have had a nice chat. Maria picked up the coffee pot and poured a cup of the thick brew, motioning Nicole to sit down at the kitchen table.

'Oh, no, thank you; I really haven't time. My patient . . .'

But Maria was insistent. Nicole decided she would have to wait for the omelette anyway, so she capitulated, smiling graciously. It was a very small cup; two sips and it was finished. She listened, fascinated, to the flow of words as the cook broke the eggs into a large bowl and whisked them vigorously. As they were being transferred to the pan, the kitchen door opened.

'Enjoying yourself, Nicole?' She recognised the sardonic, steely voice, without turning round.

'I'm waiting for an omelette,' she replied with icy calm.

'Don't bother.' Alexander strode into the room, and stood towering above her. 'Stavros has gone. While you were sitting here drinking coffee, he vanished.'

'I'm sorry . . .' Nicole began.

'So am I.' He turned on his heel and left her.

CHAPTER FIVE

FOR the next few days, Alexander seemed to be avoiding her. Nicole was glad; she was still smarting from his insinuation that it was her fault Stavros had gone away, without having eaten. They worked together in hospital occasionally, but the surgeon seemed to have delegated most of the work to his junior doctor.

'The great Capodistrias hasn't got time for us any more,' she remarked, as she helped Nikos in the out-patient department. 'I expect he's dying to go back to London.'

'Well, that was why I was appointed, but he doesn't seem to be in any hurry. Maybe he's still worried about his father; more likely he can't tear himself away from his sailing. I saw him out in that luxury yacht again yesterday. He's always in it.' Nikos grinned. 'There's a rather delightful female on board—haven't seen her close up, but from afar she looks exciting.'

'Really? What *are* you suggesting, Doctor?' Nicole's tone was deliberately light, but she felt a flicker of some unfamiliar emotion. It wasn't jealousy . . . no, it definitely *wasn't* jealousy! She didn't care how Alexander spent his time. The sooner he went back to London, the better! She moved away from the desk to prepare one of the cubicles for the next patient, whisking the curtains round with unaccustomed vigour.

'My! We are full of health and strength this morning.'

She turned at the sound of the consultant's voice. He was wearing stone coloured trousers and a cool white designer shirt, open at the neck to reveal thick dark hairs on the sun-tanned skin.

'Can I help you, sir?' Her eyes were cold as she raised them to his.

'I doubt it; not unless you're any good at sailing.' He smiled boyishly, and in spite of herself, Nicole found her pulses quickening as she looked into the brilliant green-hazel eyes. He was so maddeningly attractive! 'I just dropped in to see if you can cope without me for a few hours,' he added lightly.

'No problem, sir.' Nikos had come over to join them. 'It's very quiet this morning.'

'Yes, I didn't have many patients up at the pharmacy. No young ladies in distress.' He looked down at Nicole. 'How is the cat-bite wound?'

'Fine. It's healing nicely. I dressed it again this morning.' She held up the finger with its small white bandage.

'I'd like to take a look at it . . .' He had reached down and was already removing the dressing.

She shivered at the touch of his fingers, and the nearness of his warm body, but she remained perfectly still, willing the feeling to go away.

'That looks good. Leave it open to the air when you're not on duty.' He started to move away. 'I'll be in later this afternoon. Oh, there is just one thing you could do for me, Nicole.'

'Yes?' She watched him pulling a small envelope from his pocket. 'I meant to deliver this to Setiris' wife, but I'm late already. Could you call in to see her for me—it's on your way up the kali strata—the pink house, half-way up; you can't miss it. The balcony on the first floor juts out over the path.'

She nodded. 'I know the one you mean. They've got a lot of children and cats.'

He laughed. 'That could apply to most of the houses.

I'm very grateful. It's details of welfare arrangements and so on.'

Nicole took the envelope and put it in the pocket of her uniform. 'I'll take it at lunchtime. I'm off duty this afternoon.'

'Thanks.' He breezed out of the hospital as quickly as he had arrived.

Nicole glanced out of the window and saw that the white yacht was anchored in the harbour. A slim, elegant figure in a miniscule bikini was lying on the deck. She turned hurriedly back to her task.

It was unbearably hot as she walked away from the hospital and went down the steps to the waterside. She had changed out of her uniform and put on a pale blue cotton skirt and top, but she still felt restricted. It would be good to get away for a while. She would strip off and lie on her patio all afternoon. Bliss! But first she had to climb the kali strata.

She walked along the harbour side, smiling at the friendly people who greeted her as if she had always lived there. They recognised her, even after such a short time on the island, and she was no longer just a visitor. She was one of them. A group of young men were sitting at a table outside a taverna. They were being exceptionally noisy, and Nicole glanced across.

'Stavros!' she said his name out loud, without thinking. The young man had noticed her coming along, and was standing up, preparing to move off. She called to him.

'Don't go, Stavros.'

Reluctantly he moved away from his friends and stood in front of her. There was an inane grin on his face. She looked at the pupils of his eyes. My God! He's had another fix from somewhere.

'How are you?' she asked with a bright smile, trying to gain his confidence.

'I'm okay,' he replied sulkily.

'I wish you hadn't run off from the hospital like that; I'd prepared some food for you.'

'I wasn't hungry.' He seemed uneasy. His friends were watching him, and he wanted to get away.

'Well if you need help, you know where to come.'

He nodded and slunk back to his companions who had become ominously quiet. Nicole hoped they weren't heading for the same downward path, as she hurried towards the beginning of the kali strata. She took a deep breath as she started the ascent, unconsciously counting the steps as she went . . . ninety-nine, a hundred . . . Time for a pause, in the shade of the ruined villa that looked so elegant and reminiscent of a wealthy past. On again . . . one-hundred-and-ninety-nine . . . and here I am. Setiris' house.

A small child hovered timidly in the doorway, running inside to tell her mother that the new lady from the hospital was waiting on the step. Setiris' wife came hurrying to the door, drying her hands on her apron.

'Come in.' She smiled her welcome, and Nicole walked into the cool interior.

'Dr Capodistrias asked me to give you this.' She handed over the envelope.

'Ah, Dr Capodistrias; he is so kind . . .' the young woman said.

'It's only a few papers about . . .' Nicole began to explain.

'He takes such an interest in the people of this island —just like his father. Can I offer you a drink—some fruit juice, perhaps?'

'That would be very nice,' Nicole said gratefully. 'I'm feeling thirsty after my long climb.'

'Of course you are.'

'Your English is very good.'

'Thank you. I learned it in school, and then I travelled for a while. I became—how do you say it?—au pair for English family. Now I have my own children.' She laughed and waved her arms around the happy chaos. Three small children were playing with some kittens, an older child was helping with the washing, and a small baby gurgled in its pram outside the back door. 'My name is Zoe,' the young woman introduced herself.

'I'm Nicole.'

'But I shall call you Sister, until my husband comes home from hospital. It will be more seemly when I come to visit him.' Setiris' wife disappeared into the back kitchen to fetch the fruit juice.

Nicole smiled at the old-fashioned courtesy. Zoe can't be much older than me, she mused, and yet she seems much older, with all these responsibilities.

'Thank you.' She took a sip of the refreshing drink.

'How is my husband today?' Zoe asked.

'He's improving all the time. You'll soon have him home.' Nicole watched the lines of worry on the other woman's face.

'I hope so.' There was a poignant acceptancy of her problems that was very touching. 'And Dr Capodistrias? How is he?'

'Fine. He knows how to take care of himself.' Nicole tried to keep the bitterness from her voice.

'Such a handsome man!' Zoe sighed wistfully. 'He could have had any girl on the island, but he went away and broke all our hearts.' She gave a tinkling laugh and looked at Nicole. 'You, Sister, don't you find him attractive.'

To her embarrassment, she blushed.

'Of course you do, everyone does,' Zoe said. 'It must

be wonderful to work with him. I always wanted to be a nurse, but I could never pass all the exams.'

Nicole stood up and put the glass on a table, out of reach of the children. 'Thanks very much for the drink. I must be off now.'

'Do call in when you're passing, Sister.'

'Thank you. Goodbye, Zoe. Goodbye, children.'

The children crowded in the doorway, waving until she was out of sight round the next bend . . . Three-hundred-and-fifty . . . She was at Giorgio's Taverna. Giorgio himself came out to greet her and ask how his friend Setiris was.

'Come inside, Nicole. I make for you special tarama-salata.'

'No, thank you, Giorgio, I have to . . .'

'Sister Langley, come inside.' Yannis was walking towards her from the kitchen, a tea-towel slung carelessly across the plaster of Paris on his arm.

'I didn't know you worked here,' she said, surprised.

Giorgio laughed. 'I take pity on him. He no good to work in good restaurant, so I take him here. Plenty glasses broken already.'

Yannis grinned, and the older man patted his shoulder in a fatherly gesture before turning back to Nicole. 'What you like to drink? You are my guest. Anyone who is friend of Dr Capodistrias . . .'

Here we go again, thought Nicole, as she allowed herself to be persuaded inside.

An hour later, having tasted all the delicacies that had been forced upon her, she managed to escape, promising to return again soon.

Only a couple of hours left before I'm back on duty . . . She quickened her pace over the uneven stones and pushed open the heavy door into the lower courtyard, before climbing the steep steps to her patio. It was the middle of the afternoon hot; almost too hot to stay outside, but it would be even worse inside. As she went into her little studio apartment the temperature was unbearable. She flung wide the windows, stripped off her clothes and made for the shower. After a few minutes, clad in her smallest bikini, she relaxed in the corner of the patio, in the shade of a small olive tree.

She must have fallen asleep, because she was dreaming that Alexander had come to see her. He was looking down at her with amused eyes, and his sensuous lips were moving, as if he were trying to say something.

'So this is where you hide away in your off duty.'

She smiled in her sleep, and stretched languorously. That was exactly like his voice. So realistic . . . she opened her eyes. This was no dream! The tall figure in front of her laughed at her embarrassment.

'I'm sorry if I startled you. I had to come up to the pharmacy to see a patient, and I thought that as I was so close I would come and see what your living conditions were like. A doctor has to look after his staff, as well as his patients.' Alexander eased himself down onto the warm stones under the tree and leaned his back against the wall.

'I thought you were going sailing,' Nicole said, inconsequentially.

'I've been, but I had to return. An old woman had a heart attack, up here in the old town—nothing serious, but I've admitted her. She needs rest. Nikos is doing an ECG.'

'Perhaps I should get back.' She half raised herself from the chaise-longue.

'No, don't go. Everything's under control down there. Besides, you need your relaxation. All work and no play . . .'

His voice trailed off. 'Why do you look at me like that?'

'Like what?' she asked innocently.

'As if you were frightened of me.'

'Perhaps I am frightened of you.' She gave a small, almost imperceptible, shrug of her shoulders.

He reached up and cupped her chin in his hand. 'Don't be frightened, little one,' he said softly, and then, slowly and deliberately, he brought his lips down on hers.

She felt the pressure of that full, sensuous mouth, firm against her own for a brief second and then it was gone.

'I couldn't resist that.' Alexander's voice was husky and his eyes dazzlingly dangerous.

Nicole forced herself not to respond. Every fibre of her being cried out to be melted against that exciting, virile body, but she knew nothing could come of it. Alexander was a married man. It was no good playing with fire. She would only get her fingers burnt. With studied calm, she pulled herself off the sunbed. The stones of the patio felt warm under her bare feet. She was intensely aware of the tiny bikini she was wearing, as she faced her disturbing visitor.

'Can I get you some tea?' she asked quietly.

'Tea!' He gave a loud guffaw and reached out an arm, playfully taking hold of one of her slim ankles. 'No, I don't want tea, thank you. Perhaps some other time. I'll leave you to your siesta. See you later.'

She watched the tall figure swing easily down the stone steps to the courtyard below. The heavy wooden door banged. Oh, why did she have to have these wretched principles? Lots of people had affairs with married men nowadays. What was she thinking? If only he weren't married, it would be so wonderful! But he is, and I can't cheat on his wife, and anyway he would never leave her

for me, and I should finish up an embittered old maid
like Sister Croney . . .

Steady on! The still, small voice of reason brought her
back to her senses. One kiss and you start playing the
wronged heroine! It didn't mean anything—not to him
at any rate. He can have any woman he chooses. What
about the girl on the boat? Yes, what about *her*? She
probably doesn't care whether he's married or not, the
wanton hussy!

She laughed out loud at her ridiculous thoughts, and it
helped to release some of her tension. Nicole Langley,
you really are a fool, she told herself firmly. Put the man
out of your mind and make yourself a strong cup of tea.
Keep away from him as much as you can—he's not
worth the aggro!

It was beginning to get cool as she closed the shutters
and set off back down the kali strata.

'*Kalispéra*—good evening.' She was greeted all the
way down the narrow street by her new friends. Setiris'
children ran outside, clutching at her skirt and asked her
to come inside. Zoe waved from the doorway and told
the children to leave the Sister in peace.

The harbour was alive with early evening activity. It
was the end of the working day for most islanders, as
they sipped ouzo in the last rays of the sun.

Staff Nurse Stangos was ready to go off duty when
Nicole arrived. She had already changed into a charming linen dress, its voluminous folds hiding her ample
contours.

'You look nice, Ariadne,' Nicole told her.

'Thank you.' The nurse smiled happily. 'I'm going out
for dinner.'

'With anyone special?'

Ariadne looked sheepish. '*I* think so.'

'Lucky girl.' Best not to ask any more questions,

Nicole thought. 'Anything to report?'

'I've written it all in the book,' Ariadne told her. 'Go and see the new cardiac patient first—Kyria Popoudopolos. I don't think she's ever been away from her family before, although she's sixty-seven. Her husband is dead, but her sons and daughters have all been in. I've sent them away so she can get some rest. There's oxygen at the side of the bed, but she doesn't need it any more. She's out of danger.'

'I'll go along now. Have a nice time.'

The old lady was propped against her pillows, her eyes shut. At the sound of the opening door, she opened her eyes and gave a tired smile at the pretty young Sister.

'How are you feeling, now, Kyria Popoudopolos?' Nicole managed in Greek.

'I'm much better. The pain has gone,' the woman said. 'I don't know why I can't go home.' Mercifully, she was speaking slowly, and she had a clear voice. Nicole could understand every word.

'You need a rest, Kyria.' Nicole sat down beside her patient and took hold of the wrinkled, work-worn hands.

'No, I don't. I'm not old yet.'

Nicole smiled; Greek women didn't renounce their family commitments until they were dead. They were an integral, important part of the family. 'If you rest now, we'll soon be able to send you home.'

She checked her temperature, pulse and respiration, and was relieved to find everything normal. The old lady looked alarmed when the sphygmomanometer was produced. No-one had explained that it was just a simple way of checking her blood pressure. Nicole talked soothingly as she pumped up the column of mercury and glanced at the chart.

'That's much better than it was,' she told the patient reassuringly.

Just then the cook's assistant arrived with a tray. 'Kyria Popoudopolos!' It seemed that the young girl had known her all her life. The ensuing conversation was too rapid for Nicole.

'I'll come back later. Eat your soup.' She went out into the corridor, leaving the two friends jabbering away.

'Sister Langley, there's a phone call for you.' Nurse Vlasto was hurrying towards her.

'Thanks. I'll take it in the office.' She sank down on a chair and picked up the phone. 'Sister Langley speaking . . .'

'Nicole, my dear, how are you?'

She recognised the voice at once. 'Demetrius! Is anything wrong?'

'No; why should there be something wrong when I decide to ring a charming young lady.' The old doctor chuckled, and Nicole smiled. He hadn't lost his touch with the women. 'I've been hoping my son would bring you home again, so we could finish off our conversation, but he's so busy these days.'

Oh, he's busy, all right, Nicole thought. 'I haven't seen much of him lately.' Apart from this afternoon, which I'd rather forget!

'What time do you finish tonight?' Demetrius asked.

'Not until nine.'

'Perfect. Will you come over? I'll send the boat. I hate dining alone.' The old voice ended on a pleading note.

She couldn't disappoint him. 'I'd love to,' she told him.

'Good. Dominic will be in the harbour to meet you.'

The evening passed quickly as she settled the patients with Nurse Vlasto. Kyria Popoudopolos was perfectly happy in her little room now, and seemed to have accepted the leisured life. Just before nine, Sister Croney arrived and listened carefully to Nicole's report.

She's not such a bad old stick, after all, Nicole thought. It must be awful for her, trying to keep pace with all the changes in medical care on the island, especially if she used to be the queen bee in her youth. Now, she looks more like queen bat in that awful black uniform. I wonder if I could persuade her to change it . . . 'Dr Seferis is on call if you need him, Sister Croney.'

'What about Dr Capodistrias?' she asked sharply.

'He's off duty; emergencies only.'

The older woman sniffed. 'He seems to be permanently off duty these days.'

'I think he works at the pharmacy as well . . .' Nicole stopped. Why should she take it upon herself to defend him. If he wanted to spend all his time on the luxury yacht, that was his business. 'Good night, Sister.'

'Good night.' The black figure was already hurrying away to begin her work.

Nicole went to her room and changed into the skirt and blouse she had worn earlier. It was the only outfit she had in the room, and it was too far to trek back up the kali strata. I *must* remember to bring some decent clothes down for just such an occasion—I mean, considering I lead this wildly interesting social life!

She pattered down the steps to the harbour, soaking up the exciting atmosphere of music, laughter and fun. A couple of Greek waiters were dancing outside one of the tavernas, their arms linked across their shoulders in brotherly harmony. She paused for a few seconds to admire their sense of rhythm and intricate footwork, before hurrying on towards the silver boat which was now so familiar.

Dominic smiled as she approached, holding out a hand to help her on board. The boat moved off through the water, leaving the twinkling lights far behind as they turned into Symborio Bay. There were no other boats there. The only light came from the moon and the Capodistrias house, shining like a white, fairy-tale castle above the water.

Demetrius was sitting out on the balcony, and he waved his hand as Nicole climbed the steps from the landing stage.

Nicole waved back. He looks so lonely, she thought sadly. How inconsiderate of Alexander to neglect him like this. He might as well be back in London!

'Welcome, my dear.' The old man held out both hands towards her. 'You look charming tonight.'

Nicole smiled as she settled herself in a chair beside him. 'How are you, Demetrius?'

'I'm much better for seeing you. I get so lonely all by myself . . .'

'Doesn't Alexander stay with you at all?' she asked.

'Sometimes . . . but he has his work to do.' Demetrius was quick to defend his beloved son.

Nicole didn't want to disillusion him. 'Of course he has,' she agreed.

The old servant arrived and placed a drink on the table beside her, and she watched as he diluted it with water and ice. The liquid turned a cloudy grey. Her thoughts turned to Alexander. Where could he be at this time of night? It was much too dark to be sailing . . .

'Who's in charge of the hospital tonight?' Demetrius' voice cut through her thoughts.

'Sister Croney.'

'How do you find her?' The old eyes watched her shrewdly.

'She seems to know her job,' Nicole replied cautiously.

Demetrius breathed a sigh of relief. 'I'm glad you

think so. I thought you might find her a little—how do you say it?—old-fashioned. It isn't long before I shall have to retire her. I've already offered her a pension, but she won't hear of it. I think she's scared of retirement —won't know what to do with her time. You see, she's got no family—very sad.' The old man shook his head. 'I'm so lucky to have my family.'

When Eirene came to say that dinner was ready, he tucked his arm companiably under Nicole's and they walked slowly into the dining-room together.

Eirene had spread a white embroidered linen cloth over the long table. The silver shone, the candles were lit and there were flowers on every surface in the well polished dining-room. Demetrius motioned to Nicole to sit beside him at the head of the table.

'Kotossoupa,' he announced, as the cook brought in a large china bowl. 'Chicken soup. One of Eirene's specialities. Taste it, my dear.'

'It's very good,' Nicole said truthfully.

The cook beamed with pleasure as she returned to her kitchen to prepare the next course. When it arrived, Demetrius smiled his appreciation.

'Dominic went into Kato to buy a lobster for us. Do you like lobster, Nicole?' Demetrius looked anxiously across at his guest.

'Oh yes I do, but I haven't had it very often.'

'Let me help you to some of the more succulent . . .'

'Telephone, kirios.' Eirene was gesticulating from the doorway. The new-fangled apparatus always made her nervous. It had been installed only a year ago, and she avoided it as much as possible. If there was anyone else in the house, she let it ring.

'Answer it, will you?' the old man called, but Eirene had disappeared. He started to get up, with difficulty.

Nicole jumped to her feet. 'I'll go, Demetrius.' She

hurried out into the hall and picked up the phone.

'Thank goodness for that,' said a soft female voice. 'I thought you'd all gone away. Don't we have any servants in the house any more?'

'I'm sorry; Eirene doesn't like the telephone . . .' Nicole began.

'Who are you?' the voice cut in.

'My name is Nicole Langley. I'm dining with Dr Capodistrias tonight . . .'

'How very kind of you to answer the phone. I didn't realise . . . may I speak to Alexander—this is Vanessa Capodistrias.'

Nicole's heart missed a beat. So this was Alexander's wife. 'I'm afraid he's not here at the moment, Mrs Capodistrias. Would you like to speak to your father-in-law?' Her voice sounded calmer than she felt.

'Is he well enough to come to the phone?'

Vanessa Capodistrias seemed anxious. I expect her husband's been saying how ill his father is—that he can't possibly leave him, Nicole thought, then said, 'If you'll wait a moment, I'll see . . .'

Demetrius had appeared in the doorway. 'Who is it, my dear?'

'It's Vanessa.'

The old man took the receiver eagerly. 'Vanessa! How are you? Alexander isn't here . . .' He chatted happily with his daughter-in-law and Nicole went back into the dining-room. Snatches of the conversation drifted through . . . 'He's so busy with his work . . . you know what he's like . . . yes, I'll get him to call you . . .'

The lobster on the table no longer appealed to her. She seemed to have lost her appetite, and found the rest of the meal something of a strain. It was a relief when they got to the coffee stage. She was tired of hearing how wonderful Vanessa was, and how clever of her to cope by herself. There were lots of questions Nicole would have liked to ask about the situation, but she refrained. She looked across the drawing-room at the photographs on the piano, and decided she didn't want to know any details.

'More coffee, my dear?' Demetrius asked.

'No, thank you. I really must be getting back.' Nicole could hear voices drifting in through the open window —just like last time, except that amongst them she detected the deep mellow tones of Alexander.

'Don't go yet,' Demetrius said, 'I think my son is arriving. Stay and meet his new friends.'

This was the last thing she needed at the end of a long day but curiosity, and deference to her host, forced her to stay. Her hands were white as she gripped the side of her chair.

They were climbing the steps from the landing stage, chattering and laughing. Alexander swung easily into the drawing-room, his arm draped nonchalantly around the shoulders of a tall, slim, auburn-haired girl—quite definitely the one Nicole had seen on board the boat. There couldn't be two such poised, model-girl types out here on Ceres.

'Nicole!' For a few seconds the great Capodistrias seemed to have lost his cool. 'Whatever are you doing here? Is everything okay at the hospital?'

'What a way to greet my guest!' Demetrius remonstrated. 'I too enjoy the company of a beautiful young woman. Nicole very kindly agreed to have dinner with me.'

Alexander had regained control of himself again, and flashed the heart-melting Capodistrias smile. 'I'm so glad you came, Nicole, I don't like to leave my father alone.'

Except when you want to go out with your girl-friend, she thought furiously. 'I was just leaving . . .'

'Have a night cap with us. This is Fiona, part of the ship's crew, and Mike the captain.' The green-hazel eyes were studying her reaction, but she gave nothing away. She wouldn't give him the satisfaction of knowing how he had the power to unnerve her completely.

'Vanessa rang,' Demetrius said.

Alexander looked disappointed. 'I wish I'd been here —any message?'

'She wants you to call her.'

He nodded. 'I'll have a drink first.'

The captain of the yacht walked across and sat down near to Nicole. 'So you are the Sister at the Hospital. Do you have to work all the time or can you escape for a few hours on the sea with me?'

Alexander smiled. 'You don't waste much time, Mike.' His voice was light, but devoid of humour.

'Like your father, I enjoy the company of a beautiful woman,' he said gallantly. 'And you seem to monopolise the fabulous Fiona.'

'Oh, that's not true, Mike.' The auburn tresses shook as Fiona tossed her head, pouting in disagreement. 'Alexander is always going off to look after someone or other. Only this afternoon there was that old lady . . .'

'How is Mrs Popoudopolos?' Alexander had adopted his professional voice as he handed Nicole a drink.

'She's much better; settled in nicely. I think she needs rest more than anything, although the ECG will reveal the extent of the cardiac malfunction.'

'I'd love to be back in hospital,' said Fiona, un-expectedly.

'As a patient?' Mike grinned, and ran a hand through his curly blond hair. Nicole had been trying to decide whether it was blond or white; he couldn't be more than thirty-five or so, but it might be prematurely whitened by the sun.

'No, as a nurse. I'm SRN you know.' She squared her delicate shoulders proudly.

'I had no idea.' Alexander looked genuinely surprised. 'You've kept it very quiet.'

'I don't like to reveal all my talents at once,' Fiona said in a soft, husky voice, her eyes riveted on the surgeon.

'If you're serious, I could find you a job here, until you move on.'

Alexander was smiling down at Fiona. Nicole could imagine the expression in his eyes. She put down her glass and walked across the room to the old doctor's chair.

'It's been a lovely evening, Demetrius, but I'm very tired, so I'll say good night.'

'Good night, my dear. Dominic will take you back . . .'

'No, I'll go.' Alexander's voice was quiet but firm, and his eyes brooked no refusal.

'There's really no need . . .' Nicole started.

'I insist,' Alexander said firmly. 'Mike and Fiona will excuse me, I'm sure.'

'Of course.' Fiona was looking daggers at Nicole. 'We were going soon, anyway.'

The journey back across the water seemed endless. They were like perfect strangers, making polite conversation.

'You really didn't need to put yourself out, Alexander,' Nicole said quietly, as he steered the boat into the harbour.

'I'm not putting myself out, I assure you.' He cut the engine and leapt ashore, holding out his hand.

She reached forward gingerly and allowed herself to be helped on to the deserted quayside.

'I'd better make sure this knot is secure.' Alexander bent down towards the sturdy piece of stone, pulling hard on the rope.

Nicole's heart turned over. 'I thought you would want to get straight back.'

'I couldn't possibly leave you here all alone.'

'I'm only going to my hospital room; I don't need an escort for that.' She gave a small laugh, but he wasn't listening.

'There; that should be okay. It's a calm night.' He put an arm lightly around her shoulders—just as he had with Fiona, she remembered bitterly. He can move from one to another in the space of one evening, and his poor wife . . .

'I don't see why you can't relax, Nicole,' he said softly, drawing her against his side.

She quickened her pace. 'I'm tired—it's been a long day.'

They were climbing the steps to the hospital. Suddenly, he turned and pulled her towards him roughly. She could feel the beating of his heart through the thin cotton shirt. 'Has someone hurt you?' he asked softly.

'What do you mean?' Nicole could see the whites of his eyes in the moonlight; his mouth was parted sensuously, as if, at any moment it would swoop down and crush hers.

'You seem afraid of me—because I'm a man.'

Nicole leaned back against the stone wall at the top of the steps and studied his profile. 'You think you know everything about women, don't you . . .'

Her harsh tone surprised him. 'I don't claim anything of the sort, but I can recognise frustration when I see it . . .'

The resounding slap on his cheek surprised them both. She hadn't meant to do it, but when someone hits the nail on the head . . . 'I'm not frustrated,' she gasped angrily. 'And I haven't been hurt, either. I was engaged to someone like you for two years—it was two wasted years, as far as I'm concerned. He was married to his ambitions . . . there's no future in going out with a married man.'

His arms fell to his sides, and he took a step backwards. 'You'll get over it—in time.'

'Will I?' Her voice was shrill. 'I doubt it.' Not when she was tormented by someone like Alexander, constantly reminding her that she was a woman, who needed love and affection.

She shivered violently, and his arms were about her again. 'My poor girl.' He held her close, his mouth pressed against her tousled hair; for a few exquisite moments, Nicole contemplated how it would be if only she could melt into his arms, and then he was moving away from her.

'Good night, Nicole; sleep well.' He had paused on the bottom step.

She could see his tall, exciting profile, outlined in the moonlight. 'Good night. Don't forget to ring your wife.'

She couldn't see the expression on his face, but he sounded puzzled. 'What did you say?'

'Vanessa asked you to call her . . .'

He was laughing loudly. 'That's my sister-in-law—she was married to my brother.'

'*Was* married?' Her breathing was uneven as she peered down the steps.

Alexander stopped laughing and his tone became serious. 'My brother was killed in a car crash two years ago, just before . . .' He paused, as if searching for the right words. 'Just before things became difficult for her,' he finished, and then he was gone.

Nicole watched him running, with long athletic

strides, along the moonlit quayside. If only she could call out to him, Alexander, come back! Let's start all over again. I didn't know . . . She heard him starting the engines, heard the boat speeding across the bay, and strained her ears until there was no more sound, before she turned and went towards her lonely little room.

CHAPTER SIX

THE next few weeks were difficult for Nicole. Alexander had appointed Fiona as Staff Nurse, but the extra pair of hands seemed more of a liability than a help. Nicole found herself constantly having to check the new girl's work and she found her nerves stretched to the limit. After a particularly harrowing morning, when she had to prevent Fiona from giving twice the dosage of medicine to a cardiac patient, Nicole searched out the consultant in his room and faced him with blazing eyes.

'Either she goes—or I do,' she said with ominous calm.

'Nicole, what on earth are you talking about?' He motioned her to sit down, but she remained standing at the other side of his desk.

'I cannot be held responsible for Fiona any longer. She may be only temporary, but while she's here she's got to toe the line. She's an absolute menace. I presume you've checked her credentials . . .'

'Of course I have!' Alexander snapped. 'I've seen her certificate of State Registration from the General Nursing Council and a glowing reference from her teaching hospital . . .'

'Well, all I can say is, she seems to know less than the average nurse in Preliminary Training school!'

'My my; we're beginning to sound just like old Sister Croney, aren't we?' He moved round the desk and put his hands on her shoulders. 'Do I detect the green-eyed monster?'

'No, you do not.' Nicole shrugged away from him. 'I

simply want what's best for this hospital, and we can't afford the sort of mistakes Fiona's making.'

'Don't worry, I'll keep an eye on her . . .'

'I'm sure you will.' She hadn't meant to sound bitter, but Alexander spent so much time with the girl when they were off duty. She seemed to have bewitched him. What a man of his intelligence could possibly see in such a butterfly creature . . .

She smiled to herself. My goodness—she was becoming more and more like Sister Croney! Perhaps she was being a little harsh on the girl. It wasn't easy nursing in a small hospital like this. She'd give her another chance.

'I've got to go and start the dressings,' Nicole said. 'Perhaps you could have a word with Fiona . . .'

'I'd be delighted.' There was a tantalizing smile on his lips.

She turned quickly and made for the door. 'I'm going to have a look at Giorgios Manos, the hernia you operated on last week. The stitches should come out today, but I'm not sure about . . '

'I'll come with you.' Alexander strode across the room with long easy strides and held open the door.

Nicole's frilly cap brushed his arm as she went underneath, and she raised a hand instinctively to hold it on. 'Who designed these unpractical caps?'

He grinned. 'I think it was my father. He likes his ladies to look feminine and pretty.' He closed the door behind them and they walked down the corridor towards the surgical ward. 'I think it suits you—makes you look like a young bride,' Alexander said.

'That's what I mean.' Nicole stopped and looked up at the consultant. 'Hardly the sort of headgear for working in.'

His eyes held a gleam of amusement. 'Perhaps you would prefer to exchange with Sister Croney.'

She laughed. 'No thanks.'

The surgical patients watched as the eminent surgeon and the attractive Sister walked down between the beds. Giorgios Manos was thinking what a pleasant sight it was. They looked so well suited to each other. He wondered if there was anything going on between them. Probably not—they wouldn't have much time. Running this place must be a full time job. He remembered the morning when he'd been brought in, writhing in agony after trying to shift that huge boulder on the new villa site. He wouldn't do that again in a hurry! But the surgeon had fixed him up in no time. And nothing was too much trouble for Sister Langley.

'How are you feeling today, Giorgios?' Alexander asked.

'Fine, sir.' The patient watched apprehensively as Nicole carefully removed his dressing.

'That's much better.' Capodistrias examined the wound. 'You can take the stitches out, Sister.' Then, addressing the patient, 'Would you like to go home this afternoon?'

The young man smiled happily. 'As soon as possible —not that I want to get away from all of you—but I look forward to being with my family again.'

'Of course you do.' Nicole went over to the sink to scrub up. The consultant was still chatting to his patient when she returned. Her hands felt unaccustomedly weak as she picked up the forceps. Why doesn't he go? He's making me terribly nervous. The brilliant eyes seemed to be burning into the back of her neck, as she bent over the patient and took hold of the first stitch.

'There!' Having completed her task, she straightened her back in relief. 'That wasn't too difficult for you, was it, Giorgios?'

'Didn't feel a thing, Sister.' He looked down at his

scar. 'Nice bit of needlework there, Dr Capodistrias.'

'I'm glad you approve.' The surgeon glanced at Nicole. 'When you've finished the dressings, could you spend some time in obstetrics? That new baby isn't feeding properly, and the mother's worrying. You seem to have a knack with babies.'

'I'll do what I can.' It was all go! Switching from one department to another wasn't easy, especially when the staff weren't totally reliable.

'I'm most grateful to you.' Alexander's voice was quiet and sincere.

Nicole raised her eyes in surprise. The great man didn't hand out compliments without a reason. She wondered what was behind all this . . .

'It will be such a relief to know the hospital will be in good hands when I go back to London,' he continued.

Ah! So that was it. 'When do you plan to go?' She made herself sound casually disinterested.

'As soon as everything's under control. A couple of weeks, perhaps.'

'You're satisfied with your father's progress?' Nicole asked gently.

'Yes; he's doing fine. What do you think?'

'It's not for me to say,' she answered cagily, re-membering how he had torn her off a strip for voicing her opinion before. 'You're the doctor.'

Alexander laughed. 'Touché!' He reached forward and squeezed her hand as he went out of the door.

She gave a wry grin. It had been a brotherly gesture to him. He no longer seemed interested in her as a woman. Well, she had only herself to blame. She'd made it perfectly clear she wanted him to keep his distance. But that had been before she knew he wasn't married. And now when things might have been different she had to watch him going off with that awful phoney Staff Nurse.

Because she *was* phoney! Nicole was sure of it. Nobody as stupid as Fiona could be SRN! Thank God she was only temporary. She would probably leave when Alexander did. They're probably planning to go together . . .

She settled her patient, finished the other dressings and went off to the obstetrics room. As she pushed open the door, the noise which greeted her reminded her of the lambing season back in England—her grandparents' farm in the Welsh hills, with the tiny lambs bleating in the morning sunlight as they staggered around on spindly legs, searching for their mothers. She suffered an unexpected pang of homesickness. But where was home now? Her grandparents, who had brought her up after the death of her widowed mother, were both dead, and the farm had been sold. Her younger sister was working in the States—not far from Clark, in fact. So home was wherever her work took her.

Nicole put on a bright, reassuring smile as she went into the room. Often, the only thing she could give the mothers was confidence in themselves. This was especially so with the latest patient to be delivered. Katerina Vissos had come in during the night to have her tenth child, after several years without confinements. The other children were growing up and now there was this little afterthought to care for. He was most welcome, of course; babies were such a blessing, but at forty-five Katerina was feeling tired. And the most unpleasant thing of all was that, for the first time in her life, she couldn't feed her baby. Katerina Vissos, mother of nine large offspring, grandmother of two, felt she was a failure.

'*Kaliméra*, Kiria Vissos.' Nicole sat down beside her patient and looked at the grim face.

'I can't feed this one,' Katerina said quietly, as she

held the protesting baby to her skinny bosom.

Nicole reached forward. 'Can I hold him, Katerina?'

The mother handed over the precious bundle. 'Never before have I had one like this . . .'

'It's not the baby's fault,' Nicole put in quickly. 'And you mustn't blame yourself, either.' She soothed the crying infant with long-practised hands. 'Sometimes nature decides that it's better if the mother doesn't feed her child.'

Katerina looked puzzled, and Nicole hurried on, choosing her words carefully. 'In your case, I think you would find it very tiring to feed your little one and cope with the rest of your family . . .'

'But I fed all the others—no problem.' The dark eyes flashed resentfully.

'Exactly; but this one is different. You are different now . . . older than when you had the others. You must think of yourself this time, and conserve your strength. If it's difficult to breast feed, then we'll put him on the bottle. That way, you can have help from the rest of the family. They can all help to feed the little one.'

Whatever will she think of next, this young Sister! Doesn't she know a baby has to be fed by his mother when he is tiny. Otherwise, how will he know who is his mother? Katerina frowned and took the baby from Nicole, pressing him once more to her wizzened breast. She wanted nothing to do with these new-fangled ideas.

Nicole smiled patiently and stood up. 'I'll come back when I've seen to the others.'

Katerina nodded, almost imperceptibly, but she didn't look up at Nicole as she bent once again to her fruitless task.

Nicole went amongst the other mothers. They were all young, and feeding presented no problem. One girl was defying her family by putting her baby on the bottle, because she was flying out to America, with her husband, to visit relatives, and she'd heard that it would be difficult to breast-feed in public places. Nicole had tried to convince her otherwise, but it was no use. So, here was a mother who could breast-feed and didn't want to, and Katerina who wanted to but couldn't!

'How does she like the bottle?' She leaned over the young mother.

'She takes it very well.' The girl smiled confidently. 'It's going to be so much easier for me.'

Nicole watched for a few minutes. Out of the corner of her eye, she was aware that Katerina was watching too.

'Sister.' The older mother had swallowed her pride and decided to ask for help.

'Yes, Katerina?' Nicole was already at her bedside, wearing an encouraging smile.

'I suppose I could try the bottle, for a while—so long as it's not going to hurt my little one.' She looked anxiously at Nicole. 'What do you think, Sister?'

'I think he would do very well—and so would you. We can start him off now.' Strike while the iron is hot! 'I'll go and get a bottle.'

When she returned, Katerina was humming quietly to the hungry baby, rocking him backwards and forwards, as she had done so many times before with the others. Gently, Nicole took him from his mother and settled herself in the chair at the side of the bed. The baby gurgled softly as he took the teat in his mouth and began to suck. The mother watched, wide-eyed, almost in disbelief. Perhaps he was going to be all right after all. And it might be nice, once in a while, to let her daughters feed him – give herself a break. But she wouldn't let her husband feed the baby—nor her sons! That was unthinkable. Men didn't understand such things.

'What are you going to call him?' Nicole asked, as she

rubbed the baby's back in an effort to bring up some wind.

Katerina smiled shyly. 'I will call him Alexander, after the wonderful doctor who brought him into this world.'

'Dr Capodistrias will be flattered.' This was not the only baby to be called Alexander at the hospital. In fact, there was a positive epidemic of Alexanders, Nicole thought, as she handed him back to his mother. 'I'll come back when Alexander is due for his next feed. Perhaps you'd like to give it to him, Katerina?'

'I'll try,' was the promising reply.

It was time to go into Outpatients to help Nick, but perhaps she could snatch a quick coffee in the common room first. There were two figures out on the balcony when she got there.

'Nicole! Were your ears burning?'

'Not particularly—should they have been.' She went out and sat down beside the consultant and his friend, the captain of the yacht.

'I was asking where you were.' Mike's grey eyes swept over her appraisingly. 'Alexander said you would be too busy to break off.'

'Did you want to see me?'

'I thought it was time you came out for a sail,' he said. 'You're very elusive, you know. Every time I suggest it, you're either on duty or on call. Alexander seems to have a much more flexible timetable.'

'That's because he's the boss,' Nicole said dryly. 'And because he's not going to be out here much longer.'

'Really?' Mike sounded surprised. 'When are you going back to London?'

'It all depends,' Alexander said cryptically. 'Soon, I expect.'

'Well, in that case, we must make our beach barbecue as soon as possible. How about tomorrow? It's Sunday.

You can't be busy on Sunday.'

'We often are.' The surgeon smiled ruefully. 'Emergencies can happen on any day of the week.'

'But you've got Dr Seferis and Nurse Stangos, not to mention all the juniors . . .'

'Okay, we'll come.'

Nicole noted that Alexander had included her in his acceptance, without asking her. He was so sure of himself! 'You may have to go without me,' she said quietly. 'I've got rather a lot of things to do tomorrow . . .'

'Rubbish!' The consultant's eyes were stormy. He disliked being turned down. 'A day out on the sea will do you good. Your sun-tan is fading.'

She smiled. 'You know exactly the right thing to say to a girl.'

'I know. I've had lots of practice in persuasion,' he replied lightly.

'And does this invitation include me?' Fiona had come into the room so quietly that none of them had noticed her.

'Of course.' Alexander leapt to his feet and pulled up another chair next to him.

I wish he wouldn't make such a fuss of her, Nicole thought peevishly. I can't imagine he'll ever get around to giving her a pep talk about her work.

Fiona stretched out her long, brown bare legs, and kicked off her sandals. 'I'm exhausted already in this heat.' She turned to Nicole. 'I'd like a half day.'

'But you're down on the rota to work until five,' Nicole told her. 'You had a half day yesterday, and you've got a day off tomorrow.'

'I know; sickening isn't it!' She tossed her auburn hair out of her eyes and gave a little laugh.

Nicole swallowed hard. As far as she was concerned,

Fiona could quit the pretence of work altogether, but it was the principle of the thing. She would have to rearrange the whole duty roster.

'Any particular reason for your off duty request?' Nicole knew she was playing the heavy-handed Sister, but she didn't care, even though the men were watching her performance unsympathetically.

'I'm not feeling well,' Fiona replied, without a moment's hesitation.

'Can't you be more specific?' Nicole snapped.

'I'm afraid not, but I'll definitely need medical care this afternoon. Do you think you can come on board, Doctor?'

Alexander looked embarrassed as she leaned towards him with a sultry smile. 'Fiona, if you're going to work in the hospital, you'll have to conform to the rules . . .'

'Don't be such a pig, Alexander. I don't like keeping all these silly rules, you know that.' She pouted her lips sulkily. 'I think it's time we moved on from here, Mike. Let's go to another island.'

'No!' Surprisingly it was Capodistrias who cried out. Nicole's eyes narrowed. The girl must have bewitched him to make him so anxious for her to stay. Or did she have some kind of hold over him? It was very mysterious.

The surgeon looked calmly at Nicole. 'I think we could allow Fiona a few hours off, if she's not feeling well. After all, she's a valuable member of our team.'

'Take as much time as you like.' Nicole was seething with anger, but her voice was controlled. How could he put her on the spot like this! 'But I'd like to know in advance, if you're not going to be here.' She stood up. 'I've got to go to outpatients.'

'What about our date tomorrow?' Mike asked.

'I shall look forward to it,' she replied with a smile. 'I

hope you feel better soon, Fiona.'

She heard the brittle laughter as she closed the door.

Nick was waiting for her in outpatients. 'You took your time.' He looked hot and bad-tempered.

She would have to humour him, especially when she told him that Alexander wanted him to work tomorrow!

'What would you like me to . . .' she began.

'How about trying to stop that racket in there.' Nick waved his arm towards one of the cubicles. 'Nurse Vlasto hasn't got a clue with outpatients. Sounds as if she's murdering someone!'

'I'll take a look.' Nicole moved away briskly. 'Now, what's the problem, Nurse Vlasto?'

The young nurse raised frightened eyes from the patient to the Sister. 'She's just been brought in. Dr Seferis is too busy with another case and . . .'

'That's all right, Nurse; I'll take over.' Even from the door of the cubicle, Nicole could see she had an emergency on her hands by the deathly pallor of the young woman, the terrified features and, most disturbing of all, the tell-tale trickle of blood from under the blanket. 'Go and fetch Dr Capodistrias—he's in the common room.' She turned to the patient with a reassuring smile as she lifted the blanket.

'Please don't tell anyone, will you, Sister.' The young woman's voice was desperate. 'It's all gone wrong; I didn't know it would be like this.' She began to cry, huge racking sobs.

'Who did this to you?' Nicole asked quietly.

'I can't tell you—I promised I wouldn't.'

I bet you did, Nicole thought grimly. 'When did you have this . . .' she paused, searching for the right words '. . . this treatment?'

'Yesterday. I went to this old woman, and she did what she had to, and then she sent me away and said it would all be better in a few hours, but I started to bleed so much, and the pain . . .' She broke off as Dr Capodistrias came in.

Nicole looked up thankfully. 'Incomplete abortion,' she said in a quiet voice. 'Performed yesterday, by person or persons unknown.' The textbook jargon was the easiest description of this sort of criminal activity. It helped her to remain cool and objective about the poor, misguided patient. She could have said, 'back street abortion', but that would have been too emotive.

'Give her some Pethidine hydrochloride 100 mg to ease the pain, Sister. Then get the theatre ready; I'll do an evacuation of uterus.' He leaned over and patted the patient's hand.

'Don't tell my grandmother, Doctor,' she whispered.

'I won't, if you say who your grandmother is,' he replied easily.

'But you know her very well. It's *me*—Natalie Popoudopolos.'

The surgeon's eyes widened with surprise as he looked down at the young woman. 'I hadn't recognised you, Natalie. You've grown up since I last saw you.' He frowned. 'I thought you were getting married soon.'

'I am—but I found I was having a baby, and I worried because my family would know I wasn't a virgin when I married, so I went to see . . . to see someone who could stop the baby coming, and it was so awful . . .'

'Hush, Natalie,' Nicole whispered soothingly as she administered the Pethidine. 'Just rest quietly now.' She pulled back the blankets so that the surgeon could make his examination. All the time, she couldn't help thinking what a terrible waste it was. And all because of the strict traditions which young girls were supposed to uphold. This must be the granddaughter Kyria Popoudopolos had told her about. 'I'll go and prepare the theatre, sir.'

NO
STAMP
NEEDED

Susan Welland
Mills & Boon Reader Service
FREEPOST
PO Box 236
Croydon
Surrey
CR9 9EL

Dear Susan,

Your special introductory offer of 4 free books is too good to miss. I understand they are mine to keep together with the free Tote Bag.

Please also reserve a Mills & Boon Temptation subscription for me. If I decide to subscribe, I shall receive six new books every two months for £7.20* post and packing free. If I decide not to subscribe I shall write and tell you within 10 days. The free books and Tote Bag will be mine to keep in either case.

I understand that I may cancel or suspend my subscription at any time simply by writing to you. I am over 18 years of age.

Name _____ Signature _____

Address _____

_____

Postcode _____

*Same price as the books in the shops.   8A6TEA

YOURS FREE!

Here's the stylish shopper for the real romantic! A smart Tote Bag in natural canvas with the Mills & Boon red rose motif adding that extra touch of chic. Remember, it's yours to keep whether or not you become a subscriber.

SEND NO MONEY – TAKE NO RISKS
Mills & Boon Ltd. reserve the right to exercise discretion in granting membership. You may be mailed with other offers as a result of this application. Offer expires December 31st 1986 and is limited to one per household.

TEMPTATION

Fires at Night

ANN SALERNO

His probing, passionate kisses frightened Louise with their sensual intensity. But as he lowered her to the floor she knew she hadn't the willpower to say no . . .

Mills & Boon TEMPTATION, sensuous, provocative compelling novels that mirror today's love relationships.

Stories of passion for the woman of today – that's the key to Mills & Boon Temptation novels. Here you'll find desire and torment, rejection and revenge, described frankly and with the candour that are the hallmarks of loving and love-making in the 1980s. Now, as a regular reader of Mills & Boon Temptation novels you could enjoy six thrilling new titles every two months – delivered direct to your door, post and packing free. And by way of introduction, we will send you 4 exciting Mills & Boon Temptation novels, plus an exclusive Mills & Boon Tote Bag FREE, when you complete and return this card.

FREE TOTE BAG as your introduction to Mills & Boon Temptation

Sensuous . . . contemporary . . . compelling . . . a new romance for today's woman

TEMPTATION
Crossroads
JENNA LEE JOYCE

TEMPTATION
Another Dawn
LYNN TURNER

TEMPTATION
Love Thy Neighbour
JAN...

'Thank you. I'd like you to assist me . . .'

'Of course.' He didn't have to ask. She wanted to see this thing through with him.

'Nurse Vlasto, come and help Dr Capodistrias, please; Dr Seferis, we shall need an anaesthetist.' Nicole calmly set the wheels in motion.

Half an hour later, the emergency team was fighting to save the young girl's life. Capodistrias raised his head from underneath the bright lights above the operating table. 'We only just got her here in time. What a stupid thing to do! Will they never learn?' he said passionately.

Nicole looked across at the irate surgeon, and her heart missed a beat. His dark hair had been pushed hurriedly inside a white theatre cap, but one or two wisps had escaped above his temples. His full, sensuous mouth was covered by a mask, but the brilliant eyes shone defiantly above it. As their eyes met across the table she felt a sense of satisfaction, of achievement. It was a privilege to work with someone like this. She was going to miss him dreadfully when he went, and not just for his work . . .

She was the last person to leave the theatre. Everything had to be restored to its former pristine condition. Emergency operations were performed without warning, so the theatre had to be constantly at the ready.

'How about some lunch?'

The surgeon's voice took Nicole by surprise. She thought he had gone off duty. 'I've promised to help with a feed in obstetrics . . .'

'You need a break. Someone else can do it.'

'Yes, but I promised,' she persisted, shrugging out of her theatre gown.

He took hold of the crumpled gown in his long, sensitive fingers, and tossed it towards the laundry bin. 'You will be no good to the patients if you don't look after yourself. I'll tell Nurse Stangos to take over.' Putting his arm under hers, he led her firmly towards Reception.

'Nurse Stangos, I'm taking Sister out for some lunch, so you're in charge.'

'Is Nurse Vlasto specialling Natalie?' Nicole asked, anxiously.

The staff nurse nodded.

'Will you help Katerina Vissos to bottle feed baby Alexander? It's most important . . .'

The surgeon raised his eyebrows. 'Not *another* Alexander!'

'You should be flattered.'

'Oh, I am, but it's going to be confusing when they all start playing together in a few years' time.'

'Do you mind if I change out of my uniform?' Nicole asked. 'I feel idiotic, wandering along the quayside in this cap. It's not so much the locals, but the place is crawling with tourists in the middle of the day, and they stare as if I'm something from outer space.'

'That's only because you look so different from them. You look important, special.' Alexander's voice was husky. 'I think you're quite special, too.'

She glanced at him in surprise. 'Thank you, kind sir.' She tried to sound facetious, but the compliment had touched her deeply.

'I mean, I couldn't possibly run this place without you,' he added.

What a pity he had to qualify his remark! For a moment she had thought . . . what had she thought? Once again she'd allowed her imagination to get the better of her. 'Wait here,' she said brusquely, as they reached the door of her room. 'I'll only be a minute.'

'Don't worry; I wasn't going to invade your privacy.' His eyes held a mocking gleam as he sat down in the courtyard, under the olive tree.

When Nicole emerged, in a cool white cotton skirt and top, he smiled his approval. 'What a transformation! From weary Sister to young, attractive girl.'

She made no comment this time as he led her down the steps to the harbour, but his words had cheered her. Every time he said something like this, it made her feel that perhaps he was beginning to care for her as a woman. But then something would happen to show her that it was all on the surface. He was like Clark, incapable of deep emotion, only coming to life when he was working.

They sat down at a table outside the Oceanis Taverna, on the waterside, Marcus, the owner, came rushing outside to greet them.

'Dr Capodistrias, how nice to see you again; Sister, you are most welcome. Let me offer you an aperitif.' He waved to one of his waiters to bring the inevitable ouzo. What would you like today? We have special kefalos fish, caught this morning. I will grill it for you on the charcoal . . .'

'Sounds delicious.' Nicole smiled at the friendly proprietor.

'I agree. Make that two, Marcus. And we'll have a bottle of Ilios and some salad.'

'Of course.' The dapper little man hurried away happily to prepare the food.

'This is the sort of thing I shall miss when I'm back in London,' Alexander said, watching her with enigmatic eyes.

'Mmm,' she sighed, avoiding his eyes, as she gazed out across the water. 'It certainly beats the self-service at the Benington.'

He laughed. 'And at St Celine's. I shall miss you too, Nicole.'

'Will you? I doubt it; all those nurses fawning over

you, vying for the privilege of tying the strings on your theatre gown . . .' She broke off awkwardly, seeing the hurt look in his eyes.

'Can't you ever be serious?' Alexander asked her.

'Sometimes,' she answered glibly. When there's something to be serious about. But not with a man like you—oh, no! I've been hurt before from being too trusting.

As they ate their meal and drank their wine, they discussed the hospital, the patients, the difference between working conditions in England and Greece— anything but themselves.

At the end of the meal Alexander paid the bill.

'Thank you for lunch. I feel much better,' Nicole said.

'Of course you do.' He put an arm lightly across her shoulders and they walked back along the quayside towards the hospital. She was terribly aware of the feel of his fingers along her neckline. Did he know how distracting it was!

'Hey, Alexander! We're waiting for you.' Fiona's brittle voice floated across from the yacht, moored in the harbour.

He removed his hand. 'I won't be long; another half-hour or so.'

Nicole saw Fiona sink gracefully back on to the cushions. Nothing much wrong with her!

She had a busy afternoon, making constant checks on Natalie's condition, helping with feeds, and fitting in the other routine work. It didn't help when she saw Alexander slipping away in mid-afternoon with a casual, 'See you later, Sister.'

By the time he returned, looking sun-tanned and relaxed, she had completed the work and handed over to Sister Croney.

'I've just realised—shouldn't you have had this

evening off duty?' he asked Nicole.

Her smile was brilliant but false. 'It didn't matter. I wasn't going anywhere. Nurse Stangos wanted to go out with her boy-friend, and of course, Fiona wasn't here.'

'I'm sorry about that.' He sounded genuinely contrite.

'No need to be.' She couldn't have left Fiona in charge anyway.

'Well, you can have a whole day off tomorrow, on the yacht.'

'That'll be nice,' she said, with a shiver of apprehension. 'Will you call in to see, Natalie. She's been asking for you. What are we going to tell her grandmother? She'll have to know Natalie's in for something. Supposing they meet in the corridor . . .'

'I've been thinking about it.' Alexander smiled. 'The kindest thing would be a little white lie. We could invent an ovarian cyst.'

Nicole laughed. 'Mrs Popoudopolos will have no idea what that is.'

'Exactly! I'd hate to disillusion the dear old soul.' The consultant grinned boyishly, and Nicole felt herself drawn again to the irresistible Capodistrias charm.

'It would be bad for her condition if she ever learned the truth,' he added earnestly. 'I'll go and see Natalie, and see what she thinks.'

'Thank you. She's going to need some sedation . . .' Nicole's voice trailed away. Perhaps she was overstepping the mark again. She looked up anxiously, but his eyes were gentle.

'Go away, and stop worrying.' He reached out and cupped her chin in his hand. 'Good night, little one,' he said softly, placing a kiss on her forehead.

'Good night.' Her voice sounded strangely hoarse as she hurried away, to hide her true feelings in the velvet darkness of the Greek night.

CHAPTER SEVEN

THE early morning sun was shining on the water of the harbour as Nicole hurried down the kali strata, her canvas duffle bag swinging from her shoulder. She was wondering if she'd packed everything she was going to need for a day on the yacht. Bikini, sun-tan lotion, towel . . . She ticked them off in her mind as she acknowledged the friendly greetings. '*Kaliméra!* Yes, it is going to be hot again today.'

She was glad to be having a day off, but first she had to call in and help Nurse Stangos with the morning rush. And she wanted to see if Natalie was all right before she went.

Yesterday's emergency patient was sitting up in bed, looking relaxed and happy.

'Ah, Sister. The doctor tell me you are not coming in today.'

'I'm going off duty soon, Natalie, but I had a few things to do first. How are you today?'

'I feel well.' Her eyes took on a veiled expression. 'Did Dr Capodistrias tell you he spoke to my grandmother?'

'No; I haven't seen him yet, but we discussed it together last night, so don't worry.' She smiled reassuringly at the young woman.

'Thank you, Sister . . . for everything,' Natalie said, choosing her words carefully. 'And especially for . . . how do you say it? . . . the little white lie. I love my grandmother very much. Her generation are shocked so easily . . .'

'It was your choice, Natalie. Try to forget about it. Put it behind you, and get well. Are you going ahead with the wedding?'

'Of course.' Natalie looked surprised at the question. She was longing for the wedding day now; longing to wear her beautiful white wedding dress. Her grandmother would be so proud of her. They were to be married in the little red-domed church on the hill. And they would start another baby and this time she wouldn't have to reject it.

'Do you approve of what I did?' she asked suddenly, her eyes searching Nicole's face warily.

'Of course not,' Nicole replied harshly.

'But it was necessary . . .' the girl defended her action.

'*You* thought it was. It was extremely dangerous to put yourself at risk like that. You're lucky to be alive.'

Big tears welled in the patient's eyes. 'I didn't do it for myself, Sister.'

Nicole put her arm round the girl's shoulders. 'It's over, Natalie. Just as long as you remember never to trust an unqualified person again . . .'

'But I won't need to. I'm getting married.'

'Let's concentrate on getting you fit. Drink your medicine,' Nicole said briskly, handing over the small glass phial. 'I'm going to move this drip stand out, now that the transfusions are finished. We don't want your grandmother to know how ill you were when she comes to see you.'

'When is she coming?' Natalie sounded nervous.

'After breakfast, but don't worry. Dr Capodistrias will have prepared her . . .'

'Do I hear you taking my name in vain, Sister?' The consultant swept into the room and picked up Natalie's chart. 'Good; everything back to normal.' He smiled at his patient. 'Would you like a visitor?'

'Do you mean my grandmother?' the girl asked anxiously.

'I do indeed. She's been asking about you since early morning. I've told her all about the ovarian cyst. She's no idea what it is, so your secret is safe.' Alexander patted Natalie's hand, and she smiled up at him gratefully.

'Thank you, Doctor. You've been wonderful.'

'I thought you were off duty, Sister?' The brilliant eyes stared down at her.

'I wanted to check that everything was under control,' Nicole replied quietly.

'That was very commendable of you. But don't miss the boat.' He grinned. 'We're leaving as soon as I've briefed Dr Seferis.'

'If I'm not there you can leave without me. I'm going to feed baby Alexander before I go. Goodbye, Natalie. Nurse Stangos will look after you.'

She was half-way down the corridor before the consultant caught up with her. 'Hey, wait a minute, young lady.' He looked puzzled. 'I've no intention of going without you.'

'Give me an hour. I don't want to rush this feed.' He was standing very close to her, and her heart was beating wildly. She could handle her feelings on duty, but a whole day near that compelling body was going to be very trying.

'I'll see you down at the harbour then?'

She nodded and moved away towards Obstetrics. Katrina's face lit up and Nicole pushed open the door. She poured out a long description of Alexander's feeding habits, how he was taking the bottle well, and how easy it was for her to give it to him. Nicole smiled happily. It had been worth coming in this morning. She didn't care if the great Capodistrias did go without her!

She stayed to watch the feed, giving encouragement when the baby seemed about to fall asleep as he sucked. When everything was going well, she slipped away to change in her room. The staff quarters were deserted as she crossed the courtyard, feeling strangely vulnerable in shorts and top, after the formal uniform. She ran lightly down the steps towards the waiting yacht.

'You look much more approachable like that.' She turned at the sound of Alexander's voice behind her.

He was wearing white shorts and a cotton shirt open at the neck. The long brown, muscular legs overtook her easily. 'I got caught up with Natalie and Mrs Popoudopolos at the last minute.' He was slightly out of breath, and there was a thin trickle of sweat on his brow, dampening the dark strands of hair.

'How did it go?' She measured her steps with his as they hurried towards the yacht.

He smiled. 'Very well. They were both concerned about each other. I told Mrs Popoudopolos she can go home today, if someone will collect her. She was delighted about that, so there were no awkward questions for Natalie—just, hurry up and get well for the wedding. What a silly girl she's been!'

'She doesn't think so.' Nicole shook her head. 'You can't change centuries of conditioning in a close community like this.'

He held out his hand to help her onto the yacht. As she stepped over the side, she saw that Fiona was in her usual recumbent position on the deck cushions. 'How are you feeling today?' she asked the healthy looking figure.

'Much better, thank you, Nicole. I needed a complete rest.' She uncoiled her long, slim legs and moved across the deck towards Alexander. 'We thought you were never going to come. Where've you been?'

'Working. The patients don't disappear on Sundays, you know,' he replied curtly.

'Oh, don't be so virtuous, Alexander. Come and have a drink.' She took hold of his hand and pulled him down on the cushions beside her. 'Mike, you can tell the crew we're ready now.'

Mike appeared on deck and started issuing orders to three swarthy-looking men. Nicole decided one of them might be Greek, but the other two were of African origin.

'Best crew we've ever had,' Fiona said. 'We picked them up from another yacht on our last trip. Mike's very pleased with them.'

'What do *you* do here?' Nicole sat down on the deck near to Fiona and Alexander.

'Do? How do you mean?' Fiona looked puzzled.

'Well, I thought you were part of the crew, so what exactly is your function?' Nicole asked pointedly.

'She looks decorative,' Mike called as he threw a heavy rope on the deck.

'And I cook,' Fiona said proudly.

'*Sometimes* you cook—when it's convenient for you.'

Fiona cast a resentful glance at Mike. 'He doesn't appreciate me. One of these days . . .'

'Oh, be quiet, woman, and pour the drinks for our guests. Can't you see the rest of us are too busy.'

Fiona's face was tense with resentment, but she went down into the galley and returned with a bottle of champagne and some glasses. 'Alexander, darling. Be an angel and do the honours.'

They were sailing out of the harbour, and Nicole looked back at the view of Ceres town, nestling at the foot of the hills, its pastel and white houses spilling down

into the deep blue water. Above it the old town, domin-
ated by the monastery, seemed like some vast creation
for a film set. Alexander settled down beside her and
handed her one of the two glasses he was holding.

'Beautiful, isn't it.' He was watching her with gentle
eyes.

'Mmm.' She smiled at him, and the look he gave her
set her pulses racing again.

Fiona had noticed their closeness and was rubbing
sun-tan oil over her sleek body with unnecessary vigour.
Mike joined her, and started whispering in her ear. She
accepted his attentions, but her eyes were always on
Alexander.

The sun was already hot as they sailed along, parallel
to the rocky coast, past dark, uninhabited bays where
the sheer mountain sides fell into the sea. They nego-
tiated a narrow strait and turned into a calm, picturesque
harbour. A tiny white church sat on a piece of barren
land in the middle of the bay, joined to the mainland by a
narrow causeway.

'Ayios Emilianos—Saint Emilianos Church,' said
Mike. 'This is where we'll have our barbecue.'

Nicole helped the crew to carry the boxes of food on to
the quayside. There seemed to be enough food for an
army. Mike certainly believed in looking after his guests!
No expense had been spared. She couldn't help thinking
that he must be very rich to spend so much time sailing
around the world, with no visible source of income. It
was an expensive yacht and, presumably, the crew
would need substantial wages. She decided he must have
independent means—a rich father perhaps?

'Come and explore the island.' Alexander was smiling
down at her as she deposited one of the boxes.

'Perhaps we should help with the barbecue . . .'

'No need,' Mike said amiably. 'Fiona's a brilliant

cook, as she's already told you. Go off and enjoy yourselves.'

Fiona flashed him a withering look as she started to unpack the provisions, flanked on either side by the two Africans. 'Go and fetch the water,' she snapped at one of them. 'And open another bottle of champagne; I'm parched,' to the other.

'Yes, madame; yes, madame.'

Nicole smiled to herself at the willingness of the crew. Fiona had them eating out of her hand. They must be very well paid. She followed Alexander up the sloping rock that led to the little church. He turned to help her up the last steep incline.

'How does Mike make his living?' she asked.

He looked at the puzzled frown on her face. 'Why do you ask?'

'Just curious,' she answered lightly. 'I suppose he has a private income.'

'I expect so. Don't worry your pretty little head about it. I'm sure he can take care of himself.'

'He can always sell the yacht if he ran out of money . . .' Nicole mused.

'I don't think that's likely, but it's not your problem.' He put both hands on either side of her waist and lifted her on to the top of the rocky promontory. 'It's your day off, so relax.'

His hands remained at her waist, although she was now firmly standing in front of him. She looked up into his eyes, surprised at his grip. His mouth was parted in a mocking smile as he bent his head and brushed his lips lightly across her cheek.

'Mmm . . . I can taste the salt tang of the sea on your skin.'

She turned her head, as if drawn by a magnet, and their lips met in a long sweet kiss. Her body melted against his, moulding into the firm muscular contours as if they were made for each other. At the back of her mind, she knew it was madness to fall for someone like Alexander, but she didn't care. Her heart was ruling her head as she savoured the exquisite moment, before he pulled away, as she knew he would.

'I have to go back to London.' His voice was breathless but controlled.

'I know.' She passed a hand through her ruffled hair. He had no need to prolong the agony. If this was his way of saying goodbye . . .

'But you don't know, Nicole, and I can't explain,' he said mysteriously. 'I may have to go any day now, and there may be no chance to tell you . . .'

He broke off, as if searching for the right words. She stared at him in confusion. What was he trying to say?

'Just don't ask questions when I'm gone, Nicole. It's better if you accept it.' He took hold of her hand and began pulling her along the path to the old white church.

She followed as if in a dream, allowing him to take her into the cool interior. The painted saints and icons stared down at her from the roof and walls, as if they pitied her dilemma. They had seen it all before. A young girl, hopelessly in love with the wrong man . . .

'So this is where you got to.' Fiona had stepped into the church. 'It's a bit gloomy in here. I always think that when you've seen one of these Greek churches, you've seen them all. Come outside, Alexander; we can have a swim before lunch.'

He followed her out as meekly as a lap-dog, leaving Nicole staring up at the ornate ceiling, wishing she hadn't made her feelings so transparent.

Mike had set out the barbecue when she got back to the beach.

'That looks wonderful,' she enthused as she surveyed the cooked meats and salads. 'Do I have time for a swim?'

'Of course. Everyone else is in the water.'

'Aren't you coming in?' she asked.

'I'm feeling a bit tired—I think it's the heat.' Mike sank back on to a cushion in the shade of an olive tree.

Nicole thought he did look rather under the weather, and hoped he wasn't sickening for something. She ran into the water and swam out from the shore. Below her, she could see shoals of brightly-coloured fish swimming between the shells encrusted on the sea bed. Long trailing fingers of seaweed touched her legs as she held her breath and swam down to investigate this other world. She became fascinated by the underwater scenery and stayed longer than she thought.

'Where the hell have you been?' Alexander snapped as she ran back up the beach. 'We were worried to death.'

'I'm sorry. I couldn't tear myself away. Have you seen the fish out there? There must be . . .'

'You might have said you were going deep sea diving.' His eyes flashed angrily.

She deliberately walked away from him and sat down beside Mike. 'How are you feeling now?' she asked, concern in her voice.

'I'm still terribly hot.'

She put out a hand and felt his brow. It was wet and feverish. Her eyes met those of the surgeon in a knowing look. There was no need for words.

'Yes, I know,' Alexander said irritably. 'I've already checked him out. I think we should get back to hospital, then I can do a thorough examination. He's got a pain in the right iliac fossa.'

'It's probably nothing to worry about.' Mike shifted

uneasily. 'I've had this pain on and off for days now. It always goes away eventually.'

'I wish you'd told me. We'd better pack up and go.' Alexander was already on his feet, wrapping up the food.

'But I'm starving,' cried Fiona, reaching for a chicken joint. 'Surely we could have lunch first. I mean, whatever Mike's got can wait a bit longer.'

'We'll eat on the boat. Here, take this.' Alexander thrust a box into her hands.

Fiona and the crew ate a hearty lunch on the way back, but Alexander and Nicole hovered anxiously over Mike. He was obviously in great pain, his temperature was high and he had a rapid pulse.

'Are you thinking what I'm thinking?' she whispered to the surgeon.

'I expect so. It's a fairly classic diagnosis isn't it?'

She nodded wordlessly. Appendicitis; she'd seen it so often. But if Mike had been covering up the pain for some time now, there was no time to be lost. She'd seen a delayed case once, which had ruptured into the peritoneum, causing severe peritonitis.

'Can't you make this boat go any faster?' Alexander was standing over the crew, tight-lipped and stern. Mike had began to groan in agony, and the surgeon felt helpless without any pain-killers.

The journey seemed to take twice as long on the way back. Alexander had radioed ahead, and the ambulance was standing by on the quayside to take them the last few yards to the hospital. When they arrived, Dominic came rushing out of Casualty to help with the stretcher.

'Okay. Easy does it,' Alexander said as he moved Mike on to the examination couch. 'Let's take a look. Hold this cover back, Sister.'

The examination confirmed their suspicions.

'Prepare the theatre. Have you had anything to eat today, Mike?'

He shook his head, rolling his legs up to his chest as another severe bout of pain waved across the abdomen. The surgeon reached for the bottle of Pethidine. 'I'll give you something to help the pain.'

Dr Seferis came in, hastily pulling on his white coat. He had been snoozing in the staff courtyard during the heat of the afternoon and looked bleary-eyed and confused.

'Pull yourself together, Doctor, and go and help Sister with the theatre. I'd like to start as soon as possible, if not sooner,' Alexander told him brusquely.

The premedication had taken effect and Mike was mercifully drowsy as Dominic wheeled him along the corridor to theatre. Nicole was waiting for them with Nurse Stangos and Nurse Vlasto. Alexander was scrubbing up, but Fiona had remained in reception. She seemed to be in a state of shock, and Nicole decided that her presence in theatre would be detrimental.

'Pentothal, Sister.' Nick bent over Mike with an encouraging smile. 'Just a small injection in your arm, old man. We'll count up to ten, shall we? See how long it takes before you fall asleep. One, two, three, four, five . . . He's ready. Let's go.'

There had been no time for routine preparations, so Nicole swabbed the area where Alexander was going to make his incision.

'Sister is preparing the skin just above the level of the anterior superior iliac spine,' intoned the surgeon, falling naturally back into his role of surgical lecturer.

Nicole glanced at him with amused eyes. Anyone would think we had a gallery full of students! I guess he's already made the transition back to St Celine's in his own mind. She concentrated all her skill on the task in hand.

'Thank you, Sister. Now I'm going to make a grid-iron incision. Scalpel . . .'

The operation was routine. Nicole breathed a sigh of relief as Alexander removed the appendix intact.

'Look at that!' The surgeon held up the offending organ for everyone to see. 'Another few hours and it would have perforated causing peritonitis. Why do these patients take so long to complain of their symptoms?' He sounded tired and exasperated, and had completely forgotten that a short time before Mike had been his host.

'Perhaps he was hoping it would go away on its own,' Nicole said gently.

'That's usually the case,' Alexander agreed. 'Sutures, please. Everything all right at your end, Dr Seferis?'

Nick looked up from the breathing apparatus. 'Excellent, sir.'

Alexander carefully sewed up the wound. 'There! How do you think that looks, Sister?'

Nicole smiled her approval. 'Ever thought of taking up embroidery, sir?'

Nurse Vlasto's eyes widened in amazement above her surgical mask. This was her first operation and she had expected everything to be deadly serious. She didn't know that when doctors and nurses have to deal with matters of life and death, it's sometimes a safety valve if you can make a little joke, to ease the tension.

'Only if you'll teach me,' he replied softly. His voice was so quiet that only Nick Seferis heard it. 'Thank you, everyone.' The great Capodistrias turned to the admiring team. 'Splendid work!' He swept out of the theatre, with all the panache acquired over years of intricate surgery.

What a pity there was no adulatory crowd to witness his performance, Nicole thought bitterly. *That's why he's going back to London—to get the accolade he deserves. This place is too small for a man like that.*

She busied herself with the final clearing up after the others had gone. Plunging the steel instruments into the archaic autoclave gave her a sense of satisfaction and released some of her frustration. *The sooner Alexander went away the better!* She pulled off her theatre gown and tossed it into the laundry bin.

'I knew where I should find you.' The deep, mellow disturbing voice interrupted her thoughts.

She raised her eyes and stared coldly, at the surgeon. 'I've almost finished . . .'

'Couldn't you have delegated that to someone?' He moved towards her, a sardonic smile playing on the sensuous lips.

'No, I couldn't,' she replied firmly. 'Nurse Stangos has gone back to the ward with Mike, and I expect Fiona's playing the dying heroine scene . . .'

'You sound bitter.'

'Do I?' She flashed him a bright, spur-of-the-moment smile. 'I think I'm tired.'

'I'm not surprised.' Suddenly he was all concern. 'I've come to take you out of here. This was your day off—remember?'

'Don't worry about me. I can take care of myself,' Nicole assured him.

'We're going for a swim, and then I'll take you home for dinner,' he went on, as if she hadn't spoken. 'My father has been complaining he never sees you.'

'What about Mike?' she asked.

'Everything's under control. I've just checked him. He's fully recovered and Nurse Stangos is specialling him. Come along, young lady.' He linked his arm through hers and propelled her along the corridor towards the staff quarters.

They crossed the little courtyard and Alexander pushed open the door of her room. 'Don't be too long. It doesn't matter what you wear, but bring your bikini.'

Nicole opened the wardrobe. I'd better have a dress for dinner, but I could wear my shorts for the swimming expedition . . .

She threw on the shorts and top, crammed her white cotton dress into her duffel bag with the bikini and towel, and was back in the courtyard in a couple of minutes.

'That was quick.' Alexander smiled at her relaxed appearance. 'I'll carry that.'

She handed over her bag and ran lightly down the steps to the harbour. The heat of the day had accumulated into a heavy atmosphere at the end of the afternoon. The day trippers waited impatiently for the ferry boat that would take them back to civilisation and the comfort of their hotel bathrooms. Some of the older men sat in the shade of the tavernas sipping small cups of Greek coffee, while they discussed politics and how they were going to set the world to rights. The ever faithful Dominic held out his hand to help Nicole into the silver boat.

She marvelled at the way the young man always seemed to be in the right place at the right time. Alexander was very lucky to have such a devoted slave!

'When do you start your medical studies?' she asked, as Dominic headed the boat out of the harbour.

'That depends on Dr Capodistrias,' he replied, glancing warily at his employer.

'Yes; we've got one or two ends to tie up first,' Alexander said cryptically.

She decided not to pursue the matter, but turned her

attention towards the approaching Symborio Bay. To her relief, the white luxury yacht was nowhere to be seen.

'Where's Fiona?' she asked in an innocent voice.

'I've no idea,' Alexander answered quickly. 'The yacht isn't permanently anchored here, you know. They move around quite a lot—even without their skipper. It's a very competent crew, I believe.'

'They've gone across to Turkey,' Dominic put in quietly. 'I saw them setting out about an hour ago.'

Nicole shaded her eyes and looked across the water towards the Turkish coast. 'It's not very far, is it? I'd like to go there one day.'

'It's about three miles, but you can't go there from Greek territory.' Alexander smiled, but there was a tense look in his eyes.

'But I thought Dominic said that Fiona and the crew had gone there.'

Alexander shrugged his shoulders. 'That's their affair.'

The Turkish coast looked beautiful in the evening sunlight. Nicole wondered which of the picturesque bays was concealing the white yacht, while Fiona stretched herself luxuriously on the deck. The fact that it was forbidden territory would only increase her pleasure. Still, it was an awful risk to take, just for an evening's cruise in the sunset . . .

'Let's have a swim before we go up to the house.' Alexander helped her out on to the landing stage. 'Once my father sees you we'll have no time to ourselves.'

She glanced up at him. He made it sound as if that was the purpose of the expedition. She walked along the jetty beside him, feeling suddenly very shy.

He took her hand to help her over the rough stones, but released it when they reached the sandy cove round the corner. Nicole took her bikini from the bag and changed behind a rock. It was still damp from her morning swim at Ayios Emilianos.

'Race you out to that rock,' called a boyish voice.

She hardly recognised the transformation in the surgeon as she chased after him, laughing at his spectacular and exaggerated dive from a high boulder. Her own leap into the water was much more inhibited, but they met a few yards from the shore and swam side by side out to the small rocky island rising from the sea. She clung to the steep sides, trying to see an easy way up. Alexander reached down and gave her his hand. As she pulled her legs out of the water, she felt a sharp pain in her foot. It had scraped along the shell-encrusted wall of rock, and something had become embedded in it.

'There's something in my foot, Alexander!' She winced at the unaccustomed pain.

'Let me have a look. Keep still.'

She lay back on the warm rock and held out her foot. 'What is it?'

'It's a sea urchin. See the little black thorn sticking out of the skin?'

She grimaced. 'Is it serious, Doctor?'

'Oh, very. You'd better make a last request,' he quipped in a bantering tone. He let go of her foot and lay down beside her. 'If you live until we get back to the house, I'll remove it for you.'

'Yes, but what are you going to do now?' She ran a hand tentatively over her painful foot.

'Now?' His voice was gentle as he raised himself on to one elbow. 'There isn't much I can do at the moment, except comfort the patient . . .'

His lips moved swiftly to hers, silencing her protests. She lay very still, determined not to respond, but at the touch of his mouth her passions rose. His skin was wet with the salty sea as his broad muscular chest pinned her against the rock. She couldn't have moved, even if she'd wanted to.

'Alexander,' she murmured breathlessly, fighting to overcome her emotions, but the feel of his exploring hands on her body was too much for her. Never in the whole of her life had she experienced such a wonderful feeling of release. She was no longer in the real world, where her head ruled her heart. This was something different. She was in heaven, and there were no rules to follow here . . .

The sound of engines brought her back to earth with an unpleasant jolt. Alexander stiffened and pulled himself away. They could hear the sound of voices, Fiona's high pitched tones among them.

'We'd better get back,' he said evenly, as if nothing had happened between them.

The yacht was already in the bay, sails lowered as the crew brought it in on the engine. Alexander waved a hand to attract their attention.

Fiona spotted them and waved back. 'How romantic! Swimming in the sunset. Alexander, you certainly know how to enjoy yourself.'

'Come on, Nicole. Don't put any weight on that foot.' He was the cool, objective doctor again. 'Trust you to hurt yourself!'

The tears were pricking her eyes, threatening to mingle with the salt water of the sea as she swam back. It had been so idyllic out there, but totally removed from reality. How could she have allowed herself to be so abandoned! Heaven knows how far she would have gone if they had not been interrupted . . .

Fiona stared at her knowingly as she limped back along the shore. 'What happened to you?' she asked sharply.

'I trod on a sea-urchin.'

'That was a silly thing to do.'

'Yes, wasn't it.' Nicole met the hostile stare.

Alexander bent down to examine her foot, holding it firmly in his hand. 'Nicole doesn't have the advantage of living at sea, like you do, Fiona. I'll see to it up at the house.' He turned, putting an arm round her waist. 'Lean on me as we go up the steps.'

'Is everyone invited?' Fiona asked, moving towards Alexander.

'Not tonight, Fiona. My father gets tired very easily.'

Nicole's heart lifted as she watched Fiona swing back into the yacht. She had been trying to think of an excuse to get away early, but now she might stay on for a while.

Demetrius came out on to the balcony as they reached the top step. He smiled and waved. 'What's the matter with the invalid?'

'She's got a sea-urchin spine in her foot, Father,' Alexander explained.

'Bring her up here and we'll give her the opinion of the Academy Capodistrias. It's lovely to see you again, Nicole.' The old man's eyes twinkled merrily.

Alexander took her into his study, motioning to her to lie down on the examination couch. Demetrius wandered in and leaned over to take a look at the foot.

'I feel very safe, with two eminent doctors to look after me,' she quipped.

'Hold still, young woman, or I may have to give you an anaesthetic,' Alexander said gravely. 'Pass me the forceps, Father. Now, I want you to be very brave— there it is!' He held up the ugly black spike as proudly as he had displayed the appendix in theatre.

'What's the prognosis, Doctor?' Nicole asked.

'If the patient receives some food within the next half-hour, she stands a good chance of recovery.'

Alexander pulled her to a standing position. 'How does it feel?'

'Fine. Thanks very much.'

'I've started dinner already, but you're welcome to join me,' Demetrius said. 'Eirene will set another place. You didn't tell me you were bringing a guest, Alexander.'

'I didn't know myself until this afternoon. We had to do an emergency appendicectomy on Mike, the skipper of the yacht . . .' He launched into the technicalities of the operation, and his father listened with great interest.

'I'm afraid it's a very simple meal,' Demetrius said. 'I eat very sparingly when I'm by myself, and I never know whether my son is going to join me or not.'

Nicole smiled at the old doctor. 'It looks delicious.' She tasted some of the dolmádes, knowing already that she liked stuffed vine leaves. Eirene had cooked veal cutlets, served on a bed of lettuce and herbs, as the main course, and there was cheese and fruit for dessert.

They drank their coffee in the drawing-room which had become so familiar to Nicole. She looked at the photos on the piano, and smiled to herself when she remembered how she had mistaken Vanessa Capodistrias for Alexander's wife. It had made him so unattainable. But had anything changed since her discovery? He was still the same proud, enigmatic consultant, biding his time until he could escape back to civilisation to continue his illustrious career. How could she have been taken in by him, even for a moment!

She put her cup down on the saucer, and placed it decisively on the table. 'I must go. Thank you for your hospitality, Demetrius.'

'I'll take you back to hospital.' Alexander had sprung to his feet.

'Why don't you stay here?' Demetrius asked. 'You

can have one of the guest bedrooms, and Alexander can take you back in the morning. I'm sure you're both very tired.'

'I couldn't put you to all that trouble . . .' Nicole protested.

'It's no trouble, I assure you.' The old doctor pressed a bell. 'Eirene will show you to your room.'

As she followed Eirene out of the room she felt relieved that she wouldn't have to go back across the water in the moonlight with Alexander. She had seen the gentle look in those dazzlingly dangerous eyes, and knew how difficult it would be to resist him again!

Her room was at the front of the house, overlooking the sea. The old Greek servant moved quietly about the room, placing towels, soap, a nightdress and other essentials near at hand. When she had gone, Nicole went out on to the balcony to take a last look at the sea. The white yacht was illuminated by the light of the moon, which gave it a sinister, mysterious appearance. There was no sign of life on board. They must all have gone to sleep. Perhaps Fiona would persuade Mike to move on when Alexander went back to London. Or she might even follow him there. She was a very persistent character. When she set her mind to have something, she usually got it. Nicole shivered apprehensively and went inside.

CHAPTER EIGHT

NICOLE woke with the first light of dawn and went to the window. The white yacht was still there. Had she dreamed that she had seen Alexander creeping down to the waterside in the night? She wished it was a dream, but the reality of it came flooding back to her. It had been about an hour after she'd gone to bed. The house was still and silent, but she couldn't sleep. She had almost expected Alexander to come along to her room and tap lightly on the door. She knew she would have opened up and melted into his arms . . .

But it hadn't been like that at all. Instead, she had gone out on to the balcony for some fresh air and had seen him making his way furtively towards the yacht. As he reached it, she had gone back inside and closed the windows. She didn't want to see Fiona welcome him on board, as she inevitably would. Now, in the cold light of day, she knew she had been a fool to make her feelings so obvious. She would have been just another conquest for the great Capodistrias! It was a good thing the yacht arrived when it did, yesterday.

The rosy glow of the dawn sun was spreading across the water. It would have been wonderful to have taken a swim. But supposing Alexander had stayed all night on board? She daren't risk a confrontation down by the sea—it would be too embarrassing for both of them! She took a shower in the tiny pink and white bathroom adjoining her room, and waited until she heard movements in the house before going downstairs.

There was a delicious smell of coffee emanating from

the kitchen. She gravitated towards it and stopped dead in the doorway.

'I hadn't expected to see you here.' Even to her own ears, her voice sounded strange.

'I do live here.' Alexander stood up from the kitchen table and came to meet her. 'Why the surprise?' His green-hazel eyes were full of amusement as he gazed down at Nicole.

'It's so early,' she replied evenly.

'Yes. I've been for a swim.'

She noticed the damp hair falling over his forehead. His feet and legs were bare beneath the white towelling robe.

'Couldn't you sleep?' she asked innocently, hating herself for her duplicity.

'I like to get up early. It's the best part of the day, before it gets hot.' He turned away and went to the stove. 'Coffee?'

'Yes, please. I'll take it to my room.'

'Whatever for?' He sounded annoyed. 'Are you one of these people who has to be alone in the mornings?' He handed her the hot, steaming cup.

'Yes,' she lied.

He caught her arm gently. 'Break the habits of a lifetime, Nicole—just this once. I'd like your company.' He pulled her towards the table, and sat down. 'I don't want to be alone, not when there is a beautiful young woman in my house.'

She sat on the edge of a chair. It was always easier to go along with Alexander than to fight him, she told herself weakly. She took a sip of the strong brown liquid, and some of her former resolve returned. He may be a brilliant surgeon, but she disliked the way he handled his private life!

'I'd like to go over to the hospital fairly soon, Nicole.

There are a lot of things to attend to, today. Do you mind if we make an early start?' he said.

'Not at all. I'm ready when you are.' She was more than anxious to get out of his house and lose herself in her work.

'Half an hour, then?'

'Fine.' She watched him extricate his long legs from under the table, feeling a thrill of excitement, in spite of herself, at the sight of those brown, rippling muscles.

He stood over her for a moment, his eyes searching her face for some kind of reaction, but she remained cool and impassive to his charms. She felt his fingers brush the top of her head in a futile gesture before he went quickly out of the kitchen, almost bumping into Eirene in his haste.

'*Kaliméra.*' The cook spoke quickly in Greek, full of concern that the young doctor had made his own coffee. Then she turned her attention to the guest of the house, plying her with home-made breakfast cakes and honey.

Nicole sampled Eirene's delicacies, to be polite, but it was rather early in the day for her and she seemed to have lost her appetite. She escaped to her room as soon as she could and packed her things into the duffel bag.

The quiet knock on her door made her jump with surprise. Alexander was standing on the threshold looking cool and debonair in a dark, consultant-type suit.

'Ready?' His eyes seemed to bore into her.

Nicole stepped quickly out into the corridor before he could touch her and ruin all her resolutions. His long strides reached her and he put his arm under hers. Don't do that! she wanted to scream at him. Don't touch me! But she forced herself to walk beside him, down to the landing stage.

'It's no good offering a lift to Fiona,' he said with a wry

wanted to waste all that effort for nothing, would we? Mmm . . . that looks healthy enough. What do you think, Doctor?'

'Nice piece of embroidery.' Alexander stooped to admire his handiwork. 'Pity we have to cover it up, but I can't introduce radical techniques overnight here.'

'No point, if you're going to leave us soon,' Nicole put in lightly. 'We'll just stagger on with our ancient methods, while you enlighten the London students. They'll appreciate it.' She turned away and scrubbed her hands at the sink.

Alexander followed her. 'What's the matter, Nicole?' he asked softly. The splashing water almost drowned his voice.

'If you don't know, then I can't tell you.' She pulled the surgical mask over her mouth, wishing she could cover her eyes with it. The tears pricking behind them were threatening to flow as she bent over her patient.

'How's that?' she asked in a composed, professional voice as she completed her task.

'Looks good to me. What does the boss think?' Mike was enjoying all the attention.

'Excellent.' Alexander looked at Nicole. 'I'd like to see you in my office when you've finished,' and with that he went out of the room.

'Is something worrying you, Nicole?' Mike's eyes were shrewd as he looked up. 'You're not your usual sunny self.'

'Aren't I? Sometimes the job gets you down. For instance, the minute I got here this morning, Night Sister starts worrying me about a young patient of ours. It's so sad; he's addicted to heroin.'

'How appalling!' Mike's eyes widened in disbelief. 'I didn't know you'd get that sort of thing out here.'

'Apparently it's becoming more common. The drugs

are smuggled in on the boats.' She tried to sound un-
concerned.

'But that's wicked! If I ever caught one of my crew
with the stuff, I'd hand him straight over to the
authorities.'

'Would you, Mike?' The relief in her voice was unmistakable.

'Of course.' He laughed, then grimaced as the movement hurt his wound. 'Hey, wait a minute—You didn't
think . . . ?'

'No; it never entered my head.' Nicole plumped up his
pillows vigorously. 'I'd better go and see what the boss
wants.'

Alexander was pacing the floor in his room. 'Something's upset you, Nicole,' he said, without preamble.
'I'm not blind.'

'I'd rather not discuss it . . .' she said shortly.

'I'm sorry if . . . if I went too far yesterday. I got
carried away, in the heat of the moment. It was so
wonderful to have you to myself . . .'

'Stop it, Alexander.' Her eyes were blazing with
anger. How could he talk like this to her, having spent
the night with Fiona! He was devious, underhand and
untrustworthy. 'Forget what happened. It was all a
mistake. Let's leave it at that. It will never happen again.
Can we put it all in the past, for the sake of our
professional commitments?'

'If that's what you want,' he answered quietly.

'It is.' She faced him unsmilingly.

He turned away and walked over to the desk. 'I
promised to deliver an envelope to Setiris' wife, Zoe,
but I may not have time.' He was the cool consultant
once more. 'Would you take it for me, as you did last
time?'

'Of course.' She took the envelope from his hands

without looking at him. 'I'll take it at lunchtime.'

'Thank you.' He sat down at his desk and began to write. The painful interview was over.

Nicole went along to Obstetrics and immersed herself in helping with feeds. It never failed to cure her if she was feeling under the weather. She cuddled baby Alexander as she fed him, thinking what a pity he would have to go through life with such an unfortunate name! As she tucked him into his cot, she whispered, 'I hope you won't be as fickle as your namesake.'

Natalie was sitting beside her bed when Nicole arrived to make her comfortable.

'My, you look well! Have you been to the shower?'

Natalie nodded. 'I feel great, but I don't want to go home just yet.'

Nicole laughed. 'Well that makes a change. Most of our patients pester us to let them out. You're enjoying yourself here, I take it?'

The girl's face clouded over. 'To tell you the truth, I'm a bit scared of meeting everybody—especially my fiancé.'

'Perfectly understandable,' Nicole said briskly. 'Does he know what happened?'

'Oh yes; we discussed it together before . . . before I went ahead.'

'Well, there's nothing to worry about then. Stay a few more days, until you feel really strong.'

'Thanks, Sister. You're marvellous.'

I wish I was! Nicole thought ruefully. I wish I could solve my own problems. She bustled about the room, tidying the clothes, changing the water in the numerous vases of flowers, sent by loving relatives and friends.

It was a long, busy morning and her lack of sleep began to take its toll. She was relieved when lunchtime came

and she could hand over to Nurse Stangos. The afternoon off duty stretched ahead of her and she planned to
take a siesta, so she would be fresh for the evening's
work.

The harbour was alive with tourists browsing in the
sponge shops, haggling over the price of blankets and
buying colourful postcards to send home to their friends
. . . Wish you were here! Nicole smiled to herself. The
idea of the island was a million miles from the truth.
Underneath this dream world atmosphere, something
sinister was lurking.

She passed the Oceanis Taverna, where she had
lunched with Alexander. Glancing through the doorway, she was surprised to see his tall, unmistakable
figure. She thought he was still on duty. He was leaning
on the bar, in earnest conversation with one of the
African crew from the yacht. She paused for a moment,
wondering what the two could possibly have in common.
Then the African suddenly gave a broad smile, lighting
up his dark face, and handed over a small package.
Alexander didn't even look at it, but placed it quickly in
his pocket and walked towards the door. His head was
down, so he didn't see Nicole scurrying away along the
water-side.

What was all that about? she wondered. Her heart was
thumping away madly. Oh, please—don't let him be
involved in . . . She couldn't even bear to think about it.
Alexander Capodistrias, the great surgeon who saves
lives, accepting a package from a doubtful character who
spent his time sailing around in an area where the drug
trade was expanding. It all began to add up.

She started to hurry up the kali strata, not noticing the
heat in her haste to get away. Half-way up she was out of
breath, and had to stop.

'Nicole!' Zoe called from her doorway.

'Oh, I've got an envelope for you.' In her distress, she had forgotten.

'From the good doctor, is it? Come inside; you look hot.'

Thankfully, Nicole went into the cool interior. The children gathered round, vying for a position next to the pretty nursing Sister, but Zoe sent them away. She could see that Nicole was unusually tired and subdued.

'Let me get you a drink,' she offered.

Nicole smiled her thanks as she accepted the cold fruit juice. 'Here's the envelope. I don't know what it is this time.'

'Don't you? That's typical of Dr Capodistrias, isn't it. He doesn't like people to know when he's helping someone.' The young mother lowered her voice. 'He won't even let me tell Setiris. How we should have managed without the doctor's help, since the car crash, I don't know.'

Nicole watched, wide-eyed, as Zoe opened the envelope and pulled out a wad of hundred drachma notes. Without counting them, she put them into a heavily carved wooden box.

'Setiris thinks I'm using my savings, but they were used up long since.' She laughed vivaciously. 'With all these mouths to feed, I need all the money I can get. As soon as Setiris gets his plaster off he'll be able to start driving again, but until then, I'm dependent on the saintly doctor.'

Saintly doctor! Nicole thought angrily. Conscience money, more likely! 'He must be very rich,' she said in a matter of fact tone.

'Oh, he is, but that doesn't make it any the less wonderful that he should choose to spend his money this way. He helps anyone on the island who's in trouble.'

Zoe's eyes were shining as she extolled the virtues of the great surgeon.

I bet he does! Quite the modern-day Robin Hood! Nicole stood up. She'd heard enough to confirm her suspicions. 'Thanks for the drink. I feel most refreshed.'

And indeed she did, as she ran lightly up the last few steps of the kali strata. The revelation had given her a new sense of purpose. She couldn't wait for the evening! The confrontation with Alexander would certainly clear the air!

She pushed open the door to her apartment. Everything looked spick and span. There were fresh flowers on the table. The Greeks loved flowers. Nicole was reminded of the day she arrived at the hospital, and the romantic way in which Alexander had handed her the little blue flower . . . Forget-me-not! Oh, no; she would never forget him—and he would never forget *her*. She would see to that!

Perhaps she ought to eat something? Get her strength up for the evening! There was nothing in the fridge but a lemon and a few ice cubes. The shops would soon be closed for the afternoon . . . She ran hastily down the steps, across the little courtyard, and back into the midday heat. The baker was just putting up his shutters, but he went inside and found a couple of bread rolls. She bought some feta cheese and tomatoes in the pantopoleon—the little grocery store that seemed to sell everything from shoes to sticking plaster.

When she got back, she stretched out on her sun-lounger beneath the olive tree and savoured her spartan lunch. It tasted delicious in the open air, with the sounds of the sheep's bells drifting over from the nearby hillside, and the aroma of thyme and oregano. She felt strangely peaceful. It was the calm before the storm! Gently, she drifted off to sleep.

The air was cooler, when she opened her eyes. My goodness, I'm going to be late! That will never do —especially not tonight! She dashed into the house and put on the first thing that came to hand in the wardrobe. It was an old, comfortable catsuit in yellow crinkle cotton. She pulled on some espadrilles; they made it easy for her to run down the kali strata.

She was almost out of breath as she reached the hospital and went to her room to change into uniform. Her new-found elation seemed to have dissipated now that she was actually here. What on earth was she going to say to Alexander? Would he tell her it was none of her business? She took a deep breath; it was last-minute nerves—cold feet. Come on, Nicole; be brave! She told herself.

She listened impatiently to Nurse Stangos' report of the afternoon's work, followed by an account of the wedding reception she was going to attend that evening with her boy-friend.

'Well, you'd better get going, Ariadne . . . er, is Dr Capodistrias around?' Her voice was light and casual, but her pulses were racing.

'Oh no; I meant to tell you. He's gone,' the nurse said.

'Gone? Where to?'

Nurse Stangos was anxious to be off. 'I don't know. He's disappeared. Nobody knows where he is. Dr Seferis got a message to come back on duty this afternoon and take charge of things. Perhaps he knows what's happened. Goodbye.' She breezed out of Reception unconcernedly, her mind already on the fabulous evening ahead.

Nick Seferis in charge! Oh, no; this was too much! Nicole went down the corridor towards Alexander's office and pushed open the door.

'Don't you usually knock when you come into the

holy-of-holies?' Nick said with a broad grin. He was sitting behind the desk, reading a magazine.

'What's going on?' Nicole's face was grim as she looked at the young doctor.

'Now don't put that tone on with me, Sister.' He was still grinning, but appeared unsure of himself. 'I've been left in charge.'

'That's what I want to know about. Where is the great consultant?' Nicole asked impatiently.

'He was called away.'

'Called away?' she echoed in disbelief.

'To a conference or something.' Nick shrugged his shoulders. 'How should I know? Does it matter?'

'Yes, it *does* matter.'

He was alarmed at the intensity of her voice. 'Hey, steady on, Nicole; don't take it out on me if the boss chooses to take French leave. I just obey orders around here. All I know is that he's gone back to London. Well don't look so surprised. I mean, we knew he was going, didn't we?'

'Yes, but not like this. Not at a moment's notice!' She turned away, suddenly remembering Alexander's words when they were together at Ayios Emilianos. *'I may have to go . . . and there may be no chance to tell you . . . Just don't ask questions . . .'* She frowned as a feeling of helplessness swam over her. *'It's better if you accept it.'*

In her mind she could hear the deep, mellow voice. She owed him nothing—not after . . . But she would go along with his wishes. Maybe he had gone back because he didn't like what was happening to him out here. Whatever the reason, it was best that she wouldn't have to see him again. Perhaps one day, in the dim and distant future, they would meet again in London, and he would walk past her, trying to remember where he'd seen her before . . .

Somehow Nicole got through the evening schedule. Her mind was on automatic pilot. As soon as she had handed over to Sister Croney she made for her room in the staff quarters. There was barely time to close the door before the tears began to flow.

CHAPTER NINE

DAYS went by, and still there was no word from Alexander. Nicole threw herself into her work. Her eyes were dry; she had finished crying for the great Capodistrias! It had been inevitable, right from the start, that he would walk out on her. Surprisingly, Nick seemed to have developed a new sense of responsibility now that he was doctor-in-charge.

'I hope Capodistrias organises a replacement soon.' He was dealing with a never ending queue of out-patients, and Nicole was doing her best to ease the load for him. 'I need another pair of hands.'

'I'm doing all I can, Nick.' She put the next pile of notes on his desk. 'Setiris is here to have his plaster off.'

'See what I mean? Another doctor would make all the difference. Even an orthopaedic technician would be a help.'

'Try me,' Nicole said with a wry grin. 'I'm a dab hand with a pair of orthopaedic shears.'

'*I*'ll do the shearing, thank you, Sister,' Nick answered. 'You just bring the patient in.'

Setiris looked apprehensive when the doctor approached with a huge pair of shears.

'Don't worry.' Nicole took hold of his hand. 'He's not going to take your leg off! When do you start driving your taxi, again?' she asked, to divert his attention.

'Tomorrow.' The patient smiled happily as he watched the plaster falling away on to the floor. 'That's a relief!'

'Now, don't start any violent exercises. Take it easy

for a while,' Nicole said as she threw the old plaster in to the bin.

Setiris looked pleased with himself. 'Thanks for all your help. You will call in and see us when you're passing, won't you, Sister? My wife enjoys chatting to you and the children are always asking about you.'

'Of course I will,' Nicole said warmly. 'It's nice to have a stopping point on a hot day.'

'If ever it's too much for you, I'll give you a lift up the new road in my taxi—free of charge.' He was trying to put his foot into his shoe, with great difficulty.

'I think you'd better wear an orthopaedic slipper for a while, till the swelling goes down,' Nicole suggested. 'Wait here, Setiris; I'll go and find one. Ah, Nurse Oliver.' She had spotted Fiona sidling out of the front door. 'Could you bring me an orthopaedic shoe? I'm rather tied up at the moment.'

'Sorry, Sister. I'm just going back to the yacht. I only called in to see if Mike was okay. I've got a tummy bug, and I wouldn't want to spread it around the patients.' She gave a pathetic little smile before escaping through the door.

'That girl's more trouble than she's worth,' Nick said vehemently. 'I can't think why she was appointed in the first place.'

'Neither can I,' Nicole muttered grimly then, re-membering her patient, she put on a bright smile. 'I'll go and get your shoe, Setiris—and I might take you up on your tempting offer of a lift some time.'

When she returned with the shoe, Setiris was waiting by the door. 'You're simply dying to get away, aren't you? Sit down for a moment so I can fit this on.'

He sat down on the nearest chair. 'Truth is, Sister, I want to go and see what the opposition is like. Sergio's been back on the road for ages. It's going to be difficult getting my old customers back after all this time. It's a good thing my wife had a bit of money put by.'

'Clever girl, your wife,' Nicole said lightly. 'Now, how does that feel?'

'Great! Thanks a lot. Goodbye,' he said cheerily.

'Goodbye.' She watched him hobble down the steps for a few moments. It was always gratifying to see a patient on the road to recovery. Especially someone as nice as Setiris. She wondered how long it would be before he earned a decent income again. It would be awful if Zoe's 'savings' ran out, as well they might now that Alexander had deserted the islanders. She sighed, and went back to her work.

When all the patients had been seen, Nicole made her way along to Mike's room. He had been rather depressed for the last couple of days, and she was determined to cheer him up. It must be awful being cooped up in hospital when you are used to the open air life, she was thinking as she went in to his room.

Mike was slumped back in a chair, staring gloomily out of the window towards the sea. 'I've got to get out of here,' he announced as she came through the door. 'This place is driving me nuts.'

'Well, thank you very much. There's a grateful patient for you!' She sank down on to the side of his bed.

'Don't get me wrong, Nicole; I'm truly thankful for everything you've done, but I can't afford to stay in here.'

She glanced at him, startled by this remark. He had never shown any interest in money before, and she'd assumed that he was wealthy. What would he say if she told him that one of his crew was making a lot of money from travelling around on his yacht? Would he turn him over to the authorities, as he'd said he would? But that would only implicate Alexander . . .

'You can leave in a couple of days,' Nicole said briskly. 'I want to be sure that wound's healed before I take the stitches out. Anyway, Fiona's not well. You wouldn't want to catch her bug, now would you?'

'Stop humouring me!' Mike snapped. 'I'm not a child.'

'I'm sorry.' She had never seen Mike in such a bad temper. She leaned across to rearrange the cushion behind his head. 'Let me make you comfy . . .'

'Stop fussing, woman. Leave me alone!'

She straightened her back and retreated hastily. 'I'll come back later.' Poor Mike! He looked so untidy and unkempt. Even the strikingly blond hair was greasy and dishevelled. The roots showed through darkly—so he wasn't a natural blond after all. How strange! She'd never thought of Mike as being a vain man. His awful appearance must be getting him down, but if he wouldn't let her help him, what could she do? She went quietly out, without a backward glance, and went along the corridor to the next patient.

Natalie Popoudopolos was sitting up in bed, reading. The room was awash with flowers and cards and she was positively revelling in all the extra fuss and attention. I've got to persuade her to go home and face the real world, Nicole thought. She can't stay here for ever . . .

'You're looking well, Natalie,' she began brightly.

The patient raised her eyes from the book. 'Am I? I feel awful, Sister.'

'What kind of awful?' Nicole sat on the bed and smiled encouragingly at the young woman.

'Well, it's nothing specific—I can't put my finger on what's the matter with me.'

'I can.' Nicole spoke in a calm, quiet voice. 'You're scared.'

'Yes, I am.' The book fell on to the covers, and

Natalie burst into tears. 'I'm frightened of all the questions,' she sobbed.

'There's no need to be. All the questions have already been asked, and everyone's satisfied.' Nicole reached forward and wiped a tear away with a tissue. 'Your family want you home, Natalie, not moping in here. Aren't you excited about your wedding? Don't you want to start making plans?'

'Yes, but . . .'

'Stop making excuses.' She'd finished cajoling. It was time for some straight talking. 'I want you to get up, have a shower, and put on the clothes your mother brought. When she comes to visit you this afternoon you can go home with her. Don't look so worried— you've got to make the effort some time, and if you leave it much longer people really will start to ask questions.'

'I suppose you're right,' Natalie said reluctantly as she hauled her legs over the side of the bed. 'But can I come back and see you if I want a chat about something?'

'Of course you can—and I shall expect an invitation to the wedding!'

Natalie smiled. 'Only if you'll bring Dr Capodistrias with you.'

'Ah, well . . . that might be difficult. He's gone back to England—to a conference.'

'That's a pity. Grandma'll be disappointed—so will I,' she added with a sheepish grin. 'I think he's wonderful.'

Nicole swallowed the lump in her throat. Why was it that everyone had been taken in by him—including herself! She went into the shower room and turned on the taps.

'Come on, Natalie, get a move on,' she called brusquely. 'I haven't got all day.'

She was off duty in the afternoon, but felt too tired to

climb the kali strata. A nice quiet read in the shady
courtyard was what she needed. Nick Seferis had
already taken the prime position under the olive tree,
but he moved over to allow her some shade.

'Let me help you with your chair.' He took hold of the
unwieldy apparatus and fixed it safely on the ground.
'Try that for size, madame.'

'Thanks, Nick.' Nicole sank down on the sun-faded
cushions.

'Do I detect an air of weariness?' His shrewd eyes
swept over her lethargic figure.

'I expect you do. It's very hot.'

'Mm . . . I don't think it's just the heat. You look . . .
different. Where's the joie de vivre you used to have?'

'Where indeed?' she answered lightly.

'If I didn't know better, I'd say you were yearning for
the great Capodistrias . . .'

'Don't be silly, Nick. All I need is a bit of peace and
quiet so I can read my book, so if you don't mind . . .'

'Sorry I spoke.' He pretended to be annoyed but there
was a cunning gleam in his eye. She might be fooling
herself, but she doesn't fool me! he thought.

The long, hot afternoon droned on, enlivened by the
colourful birds and butterflies. Nick made another
attempt at conversation, but when he was severely
rebuffed he closed his eyes and drifted off to sleep.
Nicole, too, was finding the oppressive heat more con-
ducive to slumber than reading. Her eyelids felt heavy
. . . the book slipped from her hands . . .

'Oh, Sister, thank goodness you're here! I don't know
what to do about Stavros . . .'

Nicole opened her eyes and blinked up at Nurse
Stangos. 'Stavros? What about Stavros?' she was fully
awake now.

'His friend Vasiliou brought him in. He found him on

the mountain path—just above the town. We can't waken him.'

Nicole jumped to her feet. 'Did you hear . . . ?'

'Yes, I heard.' Nick was already running across the courtyard. 'Where is he?'

They found him in Casualty, lying on a trolley. A frightened Nurse Vlasto was trying to calm the hysterical Vasiliou. Nicole looked down at the still figure of Stavros, thin, emaciated and lifeless. She reached for his wrist. There was a very faint pulse. It might not be too late, after all . . .

'Tell me what happened, Vasiliou,' she asked in a gentle voice.

'He was depressed because he couldn't get another fix,' the young man answered in between his breathless sobs. 'He seemed as if he had a bad cold; his eyes were streaming, and he was shivering. I bought some aspirin at the chemist—I thought it might help him. He took the bottle from me and disappeared. I started to get worried when he didn't show up . . . Oh God, it's all my fault.'

'You mustn't blame yourself. When you found him, did he have any aspirin on him?' Nick asked anxiously.

The young man took a deep breath. 'There was an empty bottle on the path.'

'Gastric lavage—I'll get the equipment.' Nicole hurried away to the treatment room and returned with a trolley. 'Nurse Vlasto, take Vasiliou to the common room and give him a cup of tea. Dr Seferis and I can manage.' It was best to remove the hysterical element before she started the proceedings.

Stavros groaned as she inserted the rubber tube into his stomach. She smiled at Nick over the top of the funnel. 'That's a good sign. Hold his head still.'

'I've never done a gastric lavage,' the young doctor admitted quietly.

'I can see that,' she said briskly. 'Splendid! You're doing fine, Stavros. Look, he's coming round, Nick.'

Nicole finished the operation, and raised the patient's head on to a pillow. Some of his colour was returning, but he had started to shiver. She took Nick on one side.

'Do you know the history of this patient?' she asked quietly.

'Is he the drug addict?'

She nodded. 'You've seen him before, then?'

'No, but Alex briefed me on him before he left; told me to give him Methadone to reduce the withdrawal symptoms. I'll go and get some.'

As she watched Nick going off to the poisons' cupboard, she felt a sense of relief that Alexander had remembered Stavros before he went away. But then, he was always punctilious where his professional commitments were concerned.

Nicole held the young patient's hand as Nick administered the Methadone. 'You're going to be all right, Stavros,' she murmured soothingly.

The young man opened his eyes. 'Where am I?' His voice was faint and hoarse.

'Thank God!' Nicole breathed a sigh of relief. 'You're in hospital. Don't worry; we'll take care of you. I'm just going to move you into bed.'

Nick was ready to push the trolley. 'Your friend Vasiliou is here, Stavros. Would you like to see him?'

'No! I don't want to see anybody . Why didn't you let me die?' He turned his head into the pillow and started to sob. 'I don't want to live any more . . .'

'Come along, we'll get you into bed.' Nicole said gently as she nodded at Nick to move the trolley.

Nurse Stangos peeped round the cubicle. 'Is he going to be all right?' she asked quietly.

Nicole smiled encouragingly. 'Ask Vasiliou to come

along, will you? I think he might be able to help.'

Stavros remained silent and impassive as he was wheeled to his room. He allowed himself to be undressed and put into bed, as if he were a rag doll. His arms lay limply by his sides; his eyes stared unseeingly at the wall ahead.

'How are you, Stavros?' Vasiliou had come tentatively through the open door.

'Oh, it's you . . . what do you want?' Stavros turned his head towards the wall.

Vasiliou looked hurt. 'I came to see if you were better. I was the one who brought you in.'

'You stupid fool! Why didn't you leave me? What have I got to live for? I've no money! No money—no heroin! You heard what the man said . . .'

'What man?' asked Nicole.

Stavros laughed, a rasping, desperate sound. 'You don't think I'm going to tell you that, do you?'

'The man who sells the stuff . . .'

'Shut up, Vasiliou!' Stavros raised a feeble hand, as if he would strike his friend. 'If you talk, you'll find yourself at the bottom of the sea, with a stone round your neck . . .'

'Is that what he told you, this man?' Nicole knew that Stavros couldn't have made that up for himself.

'Oh, go away, all of you!' He slid down under the covers like a spoilt child and covered his head.

Nicole signalled everyone to leave. When they had gone, she settled down in a chair beside the bed and prepared to wait. She was going to get to the bottom of this. Any man who could ruin a young life like this needed stringing up! After a short while, she could hear that Stavros' breathing pattern had changed. Gently, she pulled the sheet from his face. He had fallen into a weary sleep and looked like any other teenager, free from care. She smiled with relief and pushed back the tousled black hair from his brow.

Something has got to be done for drug addicts like this! Her mind raced around in top gear. Who knows how many more young men on the island are in a similar condition? We must set up a treatment centre—facilities here are inadequate. But where will the money come from? Perhaps Demetrius will help? That might be dangerous, involving Alexander's father . . . How much did he know of what was going on?

'Can I help?' Nurse Vlasto looked in through the door.

'Sit here for a few minutes while I change into uniform will you,' she whispered. 'It must be time for me to come on duty, officially.'

'Take some time off—I'll stay on,' the nurse offered.

'No, I want to be here when he wakes up.' Nicole hurried away to her room and stripped off her unsuitable sun-dress. She had been so busy she hadn't even noticed it before, but it wouldn't do to wear it during the evening duty. Not when she had to give a report to the woman in black!

Stavros was still asleep when she got back. 'Thanks, Nurse,' she whispered as she took over. 'Would you see if you can find Nurse Stangos?'

Nurse Vlasto nodded and tiptoed out. Nicole settled down to wait. Through the window she could see the early evening sun on the water, glittering like a field of rosy red poppies. The sheep and goats on the emerald green hillside wandered aimlessly amid the sweetly-scented herbs. How could there be anything sinister on such an idyllic island? Her eyes zoomed in on the ostentatious luxury of the white yacht. Fiona was sipping a cocktail on the deck—she must be feeling better! Nicole turned back to watch her patient.

'Did you want me?' Nurse Stangos was standing in the doorway.

Nicole stood up and went out into the corridor. 'I want to stay with Stavros this evening. Can you cope with the routine work?'

'Of course. I was off this morning, so I want to get round and see all the patients,' Nurse Stangos said willingly.

'Has Natalie gone home?'

The staff nurse grinned. 'What a fuss! The whole family came—including Grandma Popoudopolos. She asked how you were, but I said you were tied up with a patient. They took Natalie home in great style.'

'Well that's a relief.'

Stavros began to stir in his bed, so Nicole went back to her chair. She took his pulse. It was stronger, but too fast. She wondered if Nick had given the correct dosage of Methadone. Drug addiction was an entirely new area to her. Obviously Alexander knew something about it. Why had he gone off, just when he was needed? Damn you, Capodistrias!

'You don't need to stay with me, Sister.' Stavros had opened his eyes.

At the sound of his grim voice, Nicole gave a start. 'I want to stay with you,' she said gently.

'To see that I don't run away?' he jibed.

'To see that you get better,' Nicole said firmly. 'What would you like for supper?'

'Not hungry.' He pulled a face.

'How about a little soup?' She was using her nursery school voice.

He shrugged, but raised himself to a sitting position.

'Well, I'm hungry even if you're not. Why don't we go along to the kitchen and see what Maria's cooking tonight?' She stood up purposefully. 'Come on, Stavros.

Don't be such a lazybones!'

For an instant he hesitated, but the new attitude of the Sister appealed to him. She mightn't be so bad, after all. 'Okay,' he muttered sullenly, putting one foot slowly on the ground.

'Here, catch this!' Nicole threw him a hospital robe, and then watched in surprise as he put it on without a murmur of protest. Maybe I'm getting through to him, she thought excitedly. 'Let's go.' Her calm voice gave no indication of her feelings. One false move and he would back off . . .

Maria smiled with delight when the young Sister walked in with her patient. From the rapid flow of words, Nicole gathered that she was to examine the numerous cooking pots and place her order. Everything looked delicious; it would be a difficult choice.

'What do you fancy, Stavros?' she asked in a matter of fact tone of voice.

'Maybe some of this soup . . .'

'My psarossoupa is the finest fish soup in the world!' exclaimed the cook, smiling all over her plump, good-natured face. 'Sit down and try some.'

'Thanks, Maria. We'd like to stay and have supper here, if that's . . .' There was no need for Nicole to ask.

'*Daxi, daxi*! Okay.' Maria bustled around, spreading a cloth over the wooden table. It wasn't often she had company in the kitchen, but then this English Sister was wonderful. A perfect match for that handsome young Capodistrias—what a pity he'd gone back to England! She placed two bowls of soup on the table and watched proudly as her guests tasted it.

Stavros was the first to speak. 'Not bad,' he pronounced in English, and grinned as he saw the puzzled look on Maria's face. He then launched into his native tongue in praise of the cooking.

Nicole smiled at the rapport between the cook and her patient. She had probably known him since he was a child. It had been a good idea to bring him along to the kitchen. He was looking so relaxed now.

'Can I have some more?' Stavros held out his bowl, and Maria hurried over to the stove. 'I didn't know I was so hungry, Sister.'

'When did you last eat?' she asked.

He shrugged. 'Can't remember.' He began to devour the second helping, and Nicole smiled gratefully at the cook.

They stayed in the kitchen for about an hour, sampling the delights of Maria's expertise. She had cooked a special souvlákia on the charcoal grill outside the kitchen door. Stavros sat on the step and watched her, just like any ordinary healthy boy.

Nicole felt a shiver of despair as she looked at him. He was caught up in a vicious circle of drugs to alleviate drugs . . . Where would it all end? she thought, as she took her patient back to his room.

'Would you like to play cards, Stavros?' Anything to keep him in a good mood.

'Okay.' He sat down on his bed, and Nicole produced a pack of cards.

The sun set outside the windows without them noticing it. Stavros was good at cards. It was something that held his interest, and he seemed to have lost some of his depression. Nicole battled on, bored by the game, but intent on winning her patient's confidence.

'So this is where you are, Sister.' The gaunt, black figure of the night sister hovered in the doorway.

'Good heavens, I didn't know it was so late! It's time you were in bed, Stavros.' Nicole picked up the cards.

'I was hoping you might come along and give me a report—don't worry,' Sister Croney said accusingly,

'Nurse Stangos has told me what's going on. Cards is it?' She sniffed in disapproval. 'Get into bed, young man.'

Stavros scowled as she bore down upon him.

'I'll see him into bed, Sister,' Nicole said quickly. 'And then I'm going to stay on for a while—just to check that he's all right.'

'There's really no need, Sister Langley. I'm perfectly capable of looking after young Stavros. I knew his poor mother, God rest her soul, and I know what she had to put up with when she was alive . . .'

'Thank you; I'll look after things here,' Nicole cut in hurriedly, before Sister Croney could destroy her evening's work. 'I won't be in your way, and you can devote your attention to the other patients,' she added in a placating tone.

'Don't go,' Stavros said quietly, 'I'd like you to stay.'

The night sister glared at the pair of them as she moved off. 'Well, I've got work to do. Cards, indeed; whatever next!' she muttered.

Stavros looked at Nicole and gave her a conspiratorial grin. 'Old battle-axe!' he muttered.

'She means well.' Nicole was quick to defend the older woman who had aroused her sense of pity on so many occasions. 'Hop into bed, now; there's a good boy.' She was back to her nursery talk. She had made progress in her relationship with the patient, but there was still a long way to go.

As she was lowering the lights Nick came in. 'I hear you're going to stay?'

She grinned. 'News travels fast around here. I suppose the black bat told you?'

He nodded. 'She disapproves, but I don't. Keep up the good work, Nicole. I'm going to bed; I'm whacked. Call me if you need me. Good night.'

'Good night,' she said softly. Her patient was almost asleep. She curled up in the chair, then suddenly remembered Mike. Perhaps it would be a good idea to see if he was all right. He'd been in such a bad mood. Wearily, she pulled herself out of the chair and padded along the corridor.

A light showed through the small window in his door; obviously he couldn't sleep. It's a good thing I came, thought Nicole.

She pushed open the door and stood rooted to the spot in surprise. He was not alone. Fiona was leaning over the washbasin, pouring liquid over Mike's head. 'What on earth!'

Fiona jumped guiltily and dropped the jug on the floor. Mike swore at her, then stopped when he saw Nicole.

'Good God, woman; I thought it was the old night sister,' he exclaimed. 'Why are you still here?' He straightened up, wincing at the pain as his abdominal muscles pulled on the stitches.

'What are you doing, Fiona?' Nicole asked with ominous calm.

'What does it look like?' the girl replied truculently. 'I'm trying to drown the old—'

'She's washing my hair,' interrupted Mike hurriedly. 'I was feeling such a mess.'

Nicole glanced at her watch. 'At midnight?' her incredulous voice displayed her disbelief. 'I take it your tummy bug has disappeared?'

'Not entirely . . .' Fiona began.

'I expect it will return in the morning,' Nicole said icily.

'Now look here, Miss holier-than-thou . . .'

'Stop it, Fiona.' Mike had grabbed her wrists as she moved in on Nicole.

'That's okay, Mike; I can handle her.' Nicole took a step towards the irate girl.

'What's going on?'

Nicole swung round as she heard the deep, mellow, voice. She must be dreaming—it couldn't be . . .

'Alexander!' The cry of delight rang from Fiona's lips as she threw herself into the surgeon's arms.

The green-hazel eyes flickered with embarrassment as Capodistrias extricated himself. 'What a welcome! I turn up at the hospital, in the middle of the night, and you're all here. How's the patient?'

'I'm fine.' Mike picked up a towel and started to rub his hair vigorously. 'Fiona's been ill all day; she was feeling better, so she dropped in to give me a shampoo.'

'That was nice of you.' Alexander smiled disarmingly at Fiona. 'Especially if you weren't well. What was the trouble?'

'I'm not sure.' Her voice was low and husky as she gazed up into his eyes. 'Maybe you could prescribe something later. Will you come back to the yacht with me, Alexander?'

'I've got work to do . . .'

'Not at midnight!' Her lips pouted in annoyance. 'Just a weeny night-cap?'

'Well, perhaps just one,' Alexander conceded.

Nicole turned away, unable to bear the intimate look in his eyes. 'I'm going back to Stavros,' she said quietly.

'Stavros? What's he doing here?' Alexander's eyes narrowed as he stared at Nicole.

'He tried to commit suicide . . .' She stopped, aware that Fiona and Mike were listening intently. 'Perhaps you'd like to come and see him?'

'Of course.' He followed her out of Mike's room and down the corridor.

As she put her hand on Stavros' door, Alexander

placed an arm on hers. 'Wait a minute, Nicole. Tell me about the patient first.'

He was trying to be professional, but the earnest gaze unnerved her. 'He took an overdose of aspirin; I've done a gastric lavage and Nick gave him some Methadone.'

'Good. How is he now?' He moved closer until she felt he must hear the rapid beating of her heart.

'He's been much better during the evening, but I don't want to leave him . . .'

Her words were swallowed as he bent his head and kissed her, gently at first, and then with an insistent pressure. 'Oh, Nicole, I've missed you so much.'

Her willing lips betrayed her as she savoured his kiss. It seemed like a lifetime since she had been in his arms. She had never thought she would ever see him again . . .

'Sister Langley! Is this why you stayed so late . . . ?' The irate night sister stood at the end of the corridor, staring in anger at the unexpected sight.

Alexander released her unhurriedly, and turned his eyes towards Sister Croney. 'I'm sure you've got work to do,' he said to the night sister in a slow, deliberate voice.

The older woman gasped as if she would explode at the rudeness of the young doctor. 'What your father would have said I do not know . . .' she was muttering as she hurried away.

Alexander laughed boyishly and reached for Nicole again, but she evaded his grasp. 'No, Alexander, be serious. I have to be with Stavros when he wakes up. He might try again—and I want to find out where he's been getting the stuff from.'

'I shouldn't do that—it's too dangerous.' Alexander sounded deadly calm.

'Why not?' She faced him with flashing eyes. 'Something's got to be done . . .'

'Stick to your nursing, Nicole,' he snapped. 'That's

what you were trained to do. I forbid you to ask any more questions. Now let's go and see the patient.'

She was trembling with anger and frustration as she pushed open the door. How dare he speak to her like that! He had no right to forbid anything of the sort.

Alexander moved quietly across the room and stood looking down at the sleeping figure. He felt for his pulse and nodded in approval.

'I'll come back in the morning when he's awake.' His eyes were cold and professional as he glanced at Nicole. Then, without another word, he swept out of the room.

She heard the sound of voices disappearing down the corridor—Fiona had caught up with him.

CHAPTER TEN

SHE was dreaming that Alexander had come back from England. He had taken her in his arms and held her close. She could smell that faint, exciting mixture of aftershave and masculine virility that set her pulses racing. But this couldn't be a dream! She opened her eyes in alarm as she felt his hand on her arm.

'I didn't mean to startle you,' he whispered, his voice husky with tenderness. 'I'll take over now.'

Nicole looked around her in confusion. Stavros was still asleep, snoring, gently as if he hadn't a care in the world. She stretched her cramped limbs and stood up.

'What time is it?'

'Something after four,' Alexander replied gently.

Her eyes widened and she looked at him properly for the first time. His clothes were crumpled, as if he hadn't changed since travelling back, and there was a pronounced dark stubble over his chin. Where had he been until the early hours of the morning? 'You look as if you need to rest, Alexander,' she said softly.

'I'm all right.' He pulled her towards him. 'You're the one I'm concerned about. You've been on duty far too long.'

'I was asleep. You should have left me . . .'

'I wanted to see you again. You looked so lovely, curled up in that chair—like a young child.' The pressure on her arms increased.

She raised her head and saw the beseeching look in his eyes. 'Trust me, Nicole,' he whispered.

'I want to . . . believe me I want to . . .'

154

There was a movement from the bed. Stavros stared at them with hollow eyes. 'Alexander; you came back!'

'I'll stay with him, Sister.' Alexander went over to the bed and leaned over his patient who grasped his hand and held on firmly, as if it were a life-line. 'Hello, Stavros.'

Nicole had been dismissed, forgotten; there was no point in staying where she was no longer needed. As she crawled into her narrow bed in the staff quarters, she remembered all the things she had wanted to ask Alexander. Where had he been? Why had he gone off without telling her? It would have to wait until she saw him again.

The sun was high in the sky when she woke to the sound of Taxiahoula's gentle humming.

'*Kaliméra.*' The young maid leaned on her broom and flashed a bright, friendly smile at Nicole. '*Kafé*?'

'*Né, parakaló.*' It still seemed strange that '*né*' meant 'yes'. She nodded her head to emphasise that yes, she did want some coffee. What a treasure this girl was!

She sipped the thick brown liquid lethargically. Yesterday had been such a long day—in fact, it had only finished at sunrise today! Perhaps that accounted for her weariness. Still, she had volunteered to stay with Stavros, so it was her own fault. And nobody would forgive her if she arrived on duty late. The routine work had to be covered.

She leapt out of bed and made for the shower, only to find that there was no hot water—it was too early in the day for the solar heating to be of any use. She shivered as she soaped away her sleepiness, but the shock had brought her brain back into action.

Once dressed, she made straight for Stavros' room and pushed open the door. Alexander lay slumped in a chair, his shirt open to the waist, revealing the sun-tanned muscular chest, covered heavily with black hairs. His long legs sprawled across the small room. She pulled in her breath. He looked so vulnerable and innocent. How could he possibly be involved in . . .

'Don't wake him, Sister.' Stavros was sitting by the window, staring out at the boats in the harbour. 'He's dead beat. I'll look after him.'

Nicole smiled at this role reversal. Stavros seemed like a different person today. Obviously Alexander was relaxed enough to fall asleep in his company. She was about to leave them to it when the surgeon opened his eyes and stared at her.

'What are you doing here?' He sounded annoyed.

'I called in to see if Stavros needed anything.'

'But I told you I would look after him. I suppose you were going to interrogate him.' He hauled himself out of the chair and stood towering above her.

'No, I wasn't!' Her eyes flashed ominously. 'I was here in my capacity of nursing sister . . .'

'Good.' Some of his easy charm had returned. 'In that case, Sister, could you instruct one of your minions to bring me some coffee?'

'Yes, sir.' Her cold, hostile tone conveyed her anger as she swept out of the door, fuming with disbelief at his arrogance.

'Nurse Vlasto, take some coffee to Dr Capodistrias.'

'Yes, Sister. Where is he?' The young nurse glanced nervously down the corridor. She wasn't used to this brusque manner.

'He's in with Stavros, of course,' Nicole snapped.

Nurse Vlasto watched curiously as the precarious cap shook with irritation. She couldn't think what she'd done wrong—Sister Langley was usually so patient with her.

Nicole sailed down the corridor as if she had a tornado behind her. He hadn't changed at all! And to think she had actually felt pleased to see him back—more than pleased! She was so engrossed with her righteous indignation that she walked straight into one of the patients coming out of his door.

'Sorry, Mike, I didn't see you!'

'That's okay.' He grinned at her in his old, happy familiar way.

She noticed he was wearing a pure silk robe and his hair looked well cared for again. The colour was staggeringly blond-white, and even from this distance she could see that the dark roots had gone. Well done, Fiona!

'I was hoping to have a word with Alexander. Have you seen anything of him this morning?'

'Yes, I've seen him,' Nicole replied shortly.

'Oh, bad as that, is it?' He laughed at her grim tone.

'He can be so infuriating!' She smiled at Mike, feeling better for having confided in someone.

'I know,' he agreed. 'I'm going to see if he'll let me out of this prison house. I've got terrible itchy feet.'

'Life on the ocean waves must be very exciting,' Nicole said. 'I can see why you hate being cooped up.'

'If he lets me out, we'll have a party on board to celebrate,' Mike said expansively.

'That would be nice.'

'Then, take me to your leader . . .'

'He's not in a very good mood,' Nicole warned. 'I don't think he's had much sleep since he got back.'

'Not to worry. Go and find him for me, Nicole, there's a darling.' He flashed her a disarming smile.

'I'll see what I can do, but I can't promise anything.'

Alexander was drinking his coffee. He seemed

surprised to see her back so soon. 'Thanks for the coffee. The service around here is very good.'

'Mike wants to see you,' she said icily.

'Is it important?'

'He wants to go home today.'

'Are his stitches ready to come out?' he asked.

'You tell me—you're the doctor.' Nicole knew she was being bloody-minded, but it was helping to get him out of her system.

'Let's go and look at him together, shall we, Sister?' Alexander's eyes shone with amusement at her display of bad temper. 'Stay here until I get back, Stavros, won't you?'

The young man nodded. 'I've got nowhere else to go,' he muttered with a sheepish grin.

'I'll give you an injection when I get back. Lead the way, Sister.' He held open the door, his arm deliberately low so that it brushed the top of her cap.

She walked away from him and then stopped in the middle of the corridor and faced him with blazing eyes. 'Nick gave him some Methadone yesterday.'

'I know; he needs a repeat dose.' Alexander's voice was calm but cold.

'I thought you were supposed to dry out drug addicts . . .'

'You don't know very much about the subject, Nicole. I've studied it at some length.'

'I bet you have!'

'What's that supposed to mean?' His eyes narrowed in consternation at her fury.

'I just hope you know what you're doing, that's all!' She moved on and went quickly into Mike's room before he could question her further.

'I've brought the big white chief himself,' she announced brightly, to conceal her anger.

'Thanks for coming, Alexander,' Mike said pleasantly. 'What's the verdict? Do I get a reprieve for good behaviour, or not?'

'Let's take a look, shall we? Lie on the bed . . .' Alexander examined the scar tissue. 'That looks healthy enough to me. Yes, the stitches can come out.' He glanced at Nicole, his eyes cool and objective. 'If you would be so kind . . . ?'

She nodded. 'Right away. And he can go immediately, can he?'

'I don't see why not,' Alexander agreed. 'Fiona's on board, presumably?'

'Yes; as you see, I have my own private nurse,' quipped Mike.

'Tell her not to come in for a few days. She's more use looking after you,' Alexander said.

She's more use anywhere than here in hospital! Nicole's spirits soared. With any luck she might decide not to come in ever again. Surely it must be time for them to move on . . .

'You're all invited to my party tonight.' Mike was in high spirits when Nicole returned with the surgical dressings trolley.

'I don't think I can make it, tonight,' Alexander said quietly.

'But you've got to come—I must have the famous surgeon who saved my life!'

'There's a lot of work to catch up on here at the hospital, and I've got to spend some time with my father . . .'

'Don't make excuses,' Mike interrupted in a bantering tone. 'We shall expect you to put in an appearance at some point in the proceedings. Fiona will be furious if you're not there.'

Alexander smiled. 'I'll see what I can do.' He was

watching Nicole's deft fingers as she removed the stitches.

She knew the surgeon was watching her, and it made her nervous, but she performed the task with mechanical skill, before raising her eyes to meet his quizzical gaze. 'Does that meet with your approval, sir?'

'Admirable! What do you think, Mike?'

'Didn't feel a thing. Thanks, Nicole.'

She collected up the instruments and pushed the trolley towards the door. 'I'll be in Obstetrics if you need me.'

'Wait a minute.' Alexander caught up with her in the corridor. 'I might need some help with Stavros.'

'Really?' Her voice held a touch of sarcasm. 'But I don't know anything about the subject.'

'Stop it, Nicole! Don't fight me over this. It's difficult enough as it is.'

'What do you want me to do?' she asked.

'Spend some time with him—he likes you. I think you've won his confidence. We've got to show him that he can kick the habit, if he wants to—but he's got to want to. The first move is to make him feel that he's a worthwhile human being. He's had a difficult life; he needs to be surrounded by caring people. Love can cure so many problems . . .'

He broke off as he gazed earnestly down at Nicole's upturned face. She was surprised at his impassioned plea. Perhaps she really had misjudged him. 'I think I get the picture,' she began softly. 'We can't cure the addiction until we remove the cause.'

'Exactly,' he breathed. 'Once Stavros has a reason for living he'll ask to be dried out, and then we can help him. It won't be easy; the withdrawal symptoms from heroin are pretty nasty, but if we supervise the operation here, he has a good chance of making it.'

'Are there any other addicts on the island?' she asked tentatively.

He paused, as if choosing the right words. 'I think it's highly probable . . . and those are the people he must stay away from if he's to kick the habit.'

'What do you know about his friend, Vasiliou? Is he okay?'

'He's definitely not an addict. I know the family well. That's the sort of boy who could help Stavros.'

'He already has.' She smiled up at Alexander's earnest expression. She loved him when he was involved in his work, like this. 'He's still here in the hospital. Shall I send him along? He's in the common room.'

'I'll go and brief him first. It's important we get this thing right.' He put his hand gently on her arm. 'And Nicole—no questions, please.'

She met his gaze with cool eyes. 'Whatever you say. You're the boss.'

The morning passed quickly in a whirl of feeds, dressings and outpatients. She had no time to brood about the surgeon's return or where he had been. Just before lunchtime she called in to see Stavros, and was pleased to see that Vasiliou was there.

'Who's winning?' She peered over their heads at the cards on the bedside table.

'Stavros, of course,' Vasiliou said with a wry grin. 'He always does. I've never known anyone who could play like he can.'

'Come on, stop talking and get on with the game, Vasiliou.' Stavros didn't even look up from his cards, but he was obviously enjoying himself.

Nicole glanced at the pile of buttons beside his hand. 'You play for high stakes, I see.'

'The doc gave us those—we haven't any money,' Stavros muttered.

Good thing too! She went out, closing the door quietly. So far so good, but it was early days. She changed out of uniform and went down into the little town. A huge cruise liner had arrived in the harbour, dwarfing the other vessels as it voided its passengers.

Nicole moved through the excited throng, trying to find a quiet taverna. The Oceanis wasn't usually busy, being so far along the waterside from the centre of activity. She stopped in her tracks as she saw the surgeon sitting outside. What on earth was he doing here, at this time? He was supposed to be catching up on his work in the hospital.

'Nicole!' He was waving to her to come over. She hoped she wasn't going to interrupt anything—she didn't want to get involved, but he was standing up now and smiling, so perhaps it would be all right.

He pulled up a chair for her beside his. 'What a pleasant surprise. Bring another glass,' he called to the waiter. 'They're cooking me an enormous fish on the charcoal. Marcus caught it this morning. Stay and have some; it's too big for one person.' He poured out a glass of cold white wine, and Nicole took a long drink to restore her confidence.

'How was England?' she asked lightly.

Alexander laughed. 'Cold, as it always is in the summer. It was a relief to get back.'

'And the conference?'

He met her quizzical eyes without flinching. 'It was most enlightening . . . ah, here's our fish. Bring another plate, please.'

The waiter hesitated as he placed the giant fish on the table. 'But I thought you say your lady is not coming today?'

Alexander spoke rapidly in Greek, and the waiter went hurriedly to the kitchen to return with a plate. 'Thank you.'

He had lost none of his charm or composure.

Nicole stared at the fish as he served her. So, he had intended to have lunch with a lady. It wasn't difficult to deduce who that might have been! She glanced across at the yacht. It wasn't like Fiona to turn down the great Capodistrias, even if she did have to minister to the sick. She wished the Greeks would remove the eyes from their fish before putting them on the table. This one was positively winking at her! Or was he in the conspiracy with the two-faced surgeon? She smiled to herself at her ridiculous thoughts. If she didn't make fun of the situation, she would start crying . . .

'You're not eating much, Nicole. Don't you like fish?' Alexander was watching her with shrewd eyes.

'I'm not very hungry. It's so hot today.' She pushed aside her plate and stared out across the dark water.

'Yes, I think there's a storm brewing. See the white flecks on the waves outside the harbour? That's a sure sign we're in for some rough weather.'

She hadn't imagined that her first social encounter with Alexander would have involved a discussion about the weather! She had dreamed about a cosy, romantic atmosphere, where he had told her that it was all a mistake, that she had jumped to the wrong conclusions . . .

'I've got to get back.' He stood up, tossing a few bank notes on to the table.

'Of course, you've got work to do.' The irony in Nicole's voice was unmistakable.

He chose to ignore it as he stood behind her chair. 'May I escort you?'

She moved away from him. 'I've got some shopping to do.'

'Then I'll see you back at the hospital.'

'I expect so.' She waited until he had disappeared into a crowd of tourists, before setting off.

The blue sky was clouding over and a strong wind blew over the water, sending a fine spray on to the tables by the harbour. Waiters were dashing around fixing their striped awnings, and the shopkeepers had moved everything inside. Only the visitors from the cruise ship appeared undeterred as they tied on their plastic rain hats.

There was no sign of Alexander in Reception when she got back. He must either be in his room, dealing with the backlog of correspondence, or in with Stavros. She would avoid both, if she possibly could.

Nicole spent the afternoon in Obstetrics. There was a new batch of mothers and babies to take care of, and all her energies were absorbed. As the rain began to lash against the window panes some of the young mothers became frightened. There was a flash of lightning, which illuminated the dark, foreboding sky, followed by a loud clap of thunder. The windows started to rattle in sympathy with the elements. Nicole went to secure them and stared through at the rising waves in the harbour. Rain-drenched tourists were scurrying back to the cruise ship, and the town was almost deserted. Mike's yacht looked safe enough but she wondered if he would cancel the party. One of the mothers started to cry.

'Don't worry, you're safe in here,' she soothed as she lifted the baby from her arms. Thank goodness the babies didn't mind the storm! She rocked the tiny scrap in her arms. 'See the pretty waves. And the big ship.' I must be mad talking to a new-born babe like this! But I think it's good for them to register words and speech, long before they understand. 'Oo, look! The big ship's going to leave us.' The loud hooter mingled with the thunder. 'I hope they've all taken their sea-sickness pills . . .'

'When you've finished amusing the babies, Sister, could you go along and see Stavros. Vasiliou has to go home, and I'm extremely busy.'

She wondered how long Alexander had been standing in the doorway watching her. He looked tense and irritable. 'Sure. I'll finish off here as soon as I can.' Nicole turned her back on him, and started to change the baby's nappy, continuing her melodious monologue as she did so. When she put the baby back in her cot, she noticed the surgeon had gone.

Busy indeed! He wasn't too busy to arrange a cosy little lunch with Fiona. Pity she didn't show up!

Stavros was waiting impatiently when she arrived. 'Where've you been? Dr Capodistrias said you were coming ages ago.'

'I do have other patients to attend to . . .' She corrected her brusque manner as she saw the scowl appear on his face. 'Sorry I took a long time to get through the work. I came as quickly as I could. Now, what would you like to do this afternoon?'

'I'm bored with cards. I'd like to go for a walk.'

'You can't walk in this weather! Just look at it!' Nicole exclaimed.

'I didn't mean by myself—you could come with me.' It was a challenge and he was watching Nicole's reaction. 'Look, the rain's stopping.'

'We could walk along the harbour, I suppose . . .' She said hesitantly.

'Yes, that would be great! Come on, Sister.' Stavros was full of enthusiasm.

'I'll have to change.'

'Thank goodness for that! You'd get blown away in the wind with that airy fairy thing on your head!'

She laughed. 'I'll be back in a minute.'

Nurse Stangos was agreeable to being left in charge, but she thought Nicole was out of her mind, and told her so.

'You don't know what these storms can be like out here!'

'We'll be okay. We're only going to walk along the harbour. You can watch us from the window, if you like.'

The staff nurse shook her head in mock despair. 'Rather you than me.'

It was like the start of a daring expedition as they went down the steps to the harbour. The wind howled around their heads and Nicole's face tingled with the beating rain.

'I thought you said the rain was stopping,' she called above the noise of the storm.

'It's not as bad as it was,' Stavros shouted, enjoying the new-found feeling of freedom.

Nicole bent her head into the wind. Although it was fierce it was warm and exhilarating. She glanced at her patient. He was grinning happily as he ploughed through the quayside puddles. It was worth the effort, she thought, as she tied the scarf more tightly round her head.

'Can we have an ice-cream?' Stavros asked suddenly. He remembered when his mother was alive she used to take him to that nice little café, jammed between the two tavernas.

'If it's open,' Nicole replied doubtfully.

There was no sign of life as they approached and then, as if by magic, the proprietor appeared and threw open the door.

'Stavros! Welcome.' He launched into rapid Greek, but Nicole got the general gist of it. He seemed to be an old friend of the family.

They chose their ice-creams from the vast display in the ice cabinet, and settled down to wait.

'I haven't been here since I was a little boy,' Stavros said quietly, looking round at the checked cloths, now faded. He remembered spilling some ice-cream on one, but his mother hadn't scolded him . . .

'I've never been in here at all. I'm glad you brought me.'

She watched him eating his ice-cream, taking a vicarious pleasure from his enjoyment. When she tried to pay the bill, the proprietor shook his head. 'You are my guests,' he said solemnly.

Nicole smiled. 'Thank you.' This happened so often on Ceres. The Greeks were the most hospitable people she had ever met.

As they trekked back through the puddles, she saw that Stavros was almost dancing. The rain had nearly stopped but the wind was stronger. They passed the white yacht and saw that everyone was below decks. The windows of the cabins were steamed up.

'Nicole!' Mike was frantically rubbing away the steam from one of the port-holes. In desperation, he flung it wide open. 'Don't be late tonight! Eight o'clock.'

'Is it still on, then?'

'Of course it is. Whyever not?' Mike grinned.

'Close the port-hole; you'll get cold,' she called automatically.

'Yes, Sister,' he replied in a pseudo dutiful voice.

She hurried up the hospital steps behind Stavros, trying to keep pace with his exuberance. He held the door open for her as they went into Reception. Nicole pulled off her scarf and shook her hair free, laughing as she felt the drips of rain running down her bare legs.

'Was it really necessary to go out in the storm, Sister?' Alexander came across the large room to meet them.

'I thought so,' she replied defensively.

'We had a great time, Doctor. You should have come with us.'

'I had work to do.' He sounded tired.

'I saw Mike; the party's still on.'

'That's nice for you, but I don't think I'll be there.' He turned away and she watched his long strides, her heart thumping madly.

'Fiona will be disappointed,' she called on impulse.

'Then perhaps I should make the effort,' he replied over his shoulder, without turning round.

Oh, the brute! She shook the rain from her coat vigorously. 'I'll go and change, Stavros. Wait for me in your room, there's a good boy.' Absent-mindedly, she had fallen back into nursery jargon.

She got through to the end of the day without any further confrontation with the enigmatic surgeon. She was even hoping that he wouldn't show up at the party. That would show Fiona what he thought of her standing him up at lunchtime!

The water was hot, in spite of the lack of sunshine, and Nicole indulged herself in a long, leisurely cascade of soap suds. 'I'm gonna wash that man right out of my hair,' she sang, as she poured the fragrant shampoo over her head.

By the time she was dressed in her new white catsuit, she felt she had exorcised away the great Capodistrias. It was so stupid of her to have fallen for him in the first place. He was a carbon copy of Clark—arrogant, two-faced, self-centred, ambitious; would she never learn! Her coat was still wet from the afternoon's escapade.

Whatever could she wear? The rain was beating down again. Perhaps Nick would lend her something.

She put a towel over her head as she ran across the wet courtyard, and knocked on Nick's door.

'Come in; you'll drown out there,' he greeted her. 'A raincoat? I've only got this old mac. It's much too big . . .'

'Thanks, Nick. I'll bring it back in the morning.' She ran back to her room.

The coat looked positively ludicrous, but she didn't care. She was going to have a whale of a time tonight, and if Alexander Capodistrias did turn up, she would ignore him. Fiona was welcome to him. They deserved each other! She tied a scarf over her newly-washed hair, belted the raincoat tightly round her waist and set off into the dark night.

CHAPTER ELEVEN

THE driving rain lashed against Nicole's face as she ran along the quayside. She could see the white yacht, shrouded in mist, bobbing precariously on the rough, foam-flecked waves. Thank goodness it's tied up in harbour! I wouldn't like to be out on the open sea on a night like this! The cruise ship had gone; Nicole hoped it had reached calmer waters by now. She shivered as she remembered the gale warnings on the hospital radio.

One of the crew hurried on deck to help her aboard. It wasn't easy to judge the heaving movements of the yacht as she scrambled in.

'Everyone is down below, madame. Come this way.'

She picked her way gingerly over the sodden deck, expecting that any moment she would be tossed into the sea. A warm fuzz of alcohol fumes emanated from the main cabin as she stepped into the lamplight.

'Nicole! My dear girl.' Mike's words were decidedly slurred as he lurched towards her. 'Have some champagne. Where's that damn steward? This bottle's empty. Bring another one.'

'Yes, sir.' It was one of the Africans who hurried away to obey the exacting master of the ship, Nicole noticed. The Greek who had helped her aboard lounged easily against the wall, as if he were one of the guests. But where was the other African—the shady-looking one who had met Alexander in the taverna and given him a package? He was nowhere to be seen. Perhaps he'd made enough money to go solo . . .

'There you go, Nicole.' Mike thrust a glass into her

hand. 'Let's have a toast to the most beautiful nursing sister who ever took my stitches out.' He raised his glass and drank deeply.

The two crew members followed suit, but Fiona remained quietly detached in a corner, staring out of the port-hole. She's waiting for him, Nicole thought. I hope he doesn't come!

The Greek was fiddling with the ship's radio, which was crackling furiously. 'There's a ship in distress. Sounds like that cruise ship . . .' he said excitedly.

'Oh no!' Nicole cried out in alarm. 'Is there anything we can do?'

Mike laughed. 'You must be joking! In a gale like this! Besides, they must be nearly at Rhodes by now. They're better equipped to deal with an emergency than we are. Switch that damn thing off. We're supposed to be celebrating.' He drained his glass noisily and reached for the bottle with an ugly scowl.

Nicole decided it would be best to humour him. 'Have you invited anyone else?' she asked politely.

'Can't remember—I expect so,' he mumbled vaguely. 'But they won't come; scared of getting wet, these landlubbers.'

'Alexander's coming.' Fiona spoke quietly, almost to herself.

'I shouldn't count on it.' Nicole knew she was being bitchy but it made her feel better! She had taken as much as she could stand from Fiona.

'He called in earlier this evening and said he wouldn't miss it for anything.'

It was tit for tat. She'd asked for it! Nicole turned away so that the other girl couldn't see her annoyance. So he was coming after all . . . the unpredictable, untrustworthy . . . I'm not going to stay and watch him flirting with that . . .

'I hope you haven't missed me too much in hospital,' Fiona said sweetly, cutting in on Nicole's thoughts. 'I'm dying to get back, but I'll have to look after Mike during his convalescence.'

'Have some more champagne.' Mike waved the bottle unsteadily over Nicole's glass.

She lifted her hand to cover the top, but Mike simply kept pouring. It was easier to remove her hand than to get wet! After the second glass, the atmosphere seemed to have eased. Even Fiona looked pleasant as she continued her vigil by the port-hole. Nicole sat down on one of the cretonne-covered bunks and leaned against the scatter cushions. She looked around her admiringly. It would be marvellous to own a magnificent vessel like this, to be able to take off at a moment's notice and sail round the world . . .

'You like my little yacht, do you?' Mike sprawled himself beside her, splashing her catsuit with champagne.

'I think it's fabulous! It must be very expensive to run—I mean, wages for the crew and everything.'

'Not really; it pays for itself . . . hey, where do you think you're taking my bottle?'

The Greek had reached across. 'You've had enough,' he growled as he moved away, carrying the champagne.

'Like hell, I have!' Mike lunged at the swarthy man and fell in a heap on the floor. 'Damn ship, always drifting up and down.'

'You're supposed to be convalescing, Mike.' Nicole looked at the pathetic figure. 'You've had far too much to drink. Here, let me give you a hand.' She leaned forward and Mike grabbed her with surprising strength, pulling her on to the floor beside him. 'That's better; give me a kiss, darling . . .'

Mike's lecherous features swam in front of her face for

barely a second before he was pushed to the other side of the cabin.

'Get up!' Alexander stood in the middle of the floor, glaring down at his drunken ex-patient.

Even Fiona looked surprised at his timely arrival. He must have appeared through the mist, when she wasn't watching. 'Alexander, don't get angry with poor Mike . . .'

'Shut up, Fiona! What's been going on in here?' The surgeon's eyes took in the whole unsavoury scene.

'We were having a quiet little drink . . .' Fiona began, in a wingeing voice.

'It looks more like a drunken orgy. I'm surprised at *you*, Nicole!' His eyes were dazzlingly hostile.

'Don't take it out on me! I was simply going to the rescue of my patient,' she flared.

'Encouraging his advances! Is that any way to——'

Her resounding slap took him by surprise. He rubbed his cheek, stunned by the force of her wrath. 'Two can play at that, my girl.' He grabbed her arms and pulled her towards him.

'Atta girl!' Mike shouted as Nicole struggled against Alexander. His loud cries drowned the sound of the surgeon's urgent whisper. 'We've got to get out of here, before it's too late.'

She glanced up at his face, but the enigmatic eyes gave nothing away. 'I'd like to go home,' she said quickly.

'I think you'd better,' Alexander agreed. 'Where's your coat?'

'You can't go now. The party's only just begun.' Mike swayed unsteadily to his feet, hanging on desperately to the edge of the table. 'You're not going as well, Alexander . . . ?'

'I can't let Nicole go back by herself, in this storm.' He put his arm protectively round her shoulders.

'But one of the crew can take her . . .'

'No, *I'll* take her.' Alexander's voice was firm as he inched his way towards the door.

'Just a minute!' The Greek stood in the doorway, barring their exit. 'I remember your voice, Dr Capodistrias. You can't fool me!'

As the Greek moved towards Alexander, Nicole felt herself pushed towards the door. 'Go! I'll follow!'

She obeyed the terse instructions in a state of wild panic. There was no way of knowing what was going on, but it was something sinister and incomprehensible, and Alexander had said they had to escape. The deck was slippery and she almost slithered into the dark water as she flung herself on to the quayside, crouching in the shadows to wait. The rain was soaking her thin cotton catsuit—there hadn't been time to put Nick's coat on. Oh, where was Alexander?

And then she saw him emerge, his arm round Fiona's shoulders. 'Don't worry, Alexander, I'll sort him out for you. I had to sack the other one because he became too big for his boots.' She turned her face towards him, and he kissed her lightly on the cheek.

'Goodbye, Fiona.' He jumped off the yacht, landing a few feet from Nicole.

'Don't you mean "Au revoir"?' Fiona called after him, but Alexander ignored her.

Reaching for Nicole's hand in the darkness he whispered, 'I most definitely mean goodbye.' He pulled her towards him with frightening urgency. 'Well done, little one. Let's go!'

They ran along the deserted quayside, through the all-enveloping mist to the steps. His hand supported her in the middle of her back as she climbed quickly up to the safety of the hospital.

She leaned against the wall inside Reception and

breathed a sigh of relief. 'What was all that about?'

'I'll explain later, but first we've got to get you out of your wet things. This way, young lady.' He took her firmly by the arm past the reception desk.

Sister Croney looked up briefly from her report and averted her eyes. *Such goings-on! She looks as if she's been swimming in her clothes!*

'How's Stavros, Sister?' Alexander asked, flashing the older woman one of his winning smiles.

He looks so much like his father when he does that! she thought fondly. There was a twinkle in her eyes as she replied, 'He's asleep, Doctor. I shouldn't disturb him if I were you.'

'I wasn't going to. I've got more urgent matters to attend to.' He glanced at Nicole and she blushed under the scrutiny of the night sister.

She started to walk away, but Alexander's arm was round her waist. Her legs felt weak as they moved down the long corridor together. They crossed the courtyard to her room; she paused on the step, and looked up at him shyly.

'You're not going to turn me away on a night like this!' he remonstrated.

'I should do,' she replied, trying to sound convincing. 'But I want to ask you a few questions.'

'That makes two of us.' He pushed open the door decisively.

Nicole turned to face him, her eyes searching his. 'I want to know . . .'

'Go and strip off your wet things, then we'll talk,' he interrupted. He sat down, nonchalantly, his back to the shower room.

She was intensely aware of him as she struggled into the tiny cubicle. It was so embarrassing to have him in the room, only a few feet away. As the warm water flooded over her she remembered her resolutions, made only a short time ago . . . but so much had happened since then. He turned to look at her as she came out, clad in a soft white towelling robe.

'Come over here.' His voice was husky as he patted the seat beside him.

She moved across the room in a dream.

'I've been looking at your flower collection,' he said softly. 'I recognise this one.' It was the forget-me-not he had given her on the first day. 'I'm glad you kept it.'

'There were times when I wanted to throw it away,' Nicole told him.

He stared at her, alarmed at the toughness in her voice. 'But you thought better of it . . .'

'Don't keep me in suspense, Alexander. I've waited so long to hear your explanation.'

He smiled and reached for her hand. 'My poor girl. Has it been so bad?' he said gently.

'It's been awful, not knowing where you were or what you were doing.'

'You look delightful when you're cross.' His hands reached out to cup her chin. 'Like a truculent child who needs spanking!'

'Don't you dare . . .' she began, laughingly, but his lips silenced her as he pulled her roughly towards him. At first, she struggled; he wasn't going to get off so easily. He had to give her some answers first . . .

The feel of his hands on her body, stroking the skin beneath her robe, sent a tingling sensation down her spine.

'No, Alexander,' she murmured feebly, but even as she said it she knew she was a slave to this maddeningly desirable man. Suddenly it seemed unimportant to understand what was going on. She was here in his arms; the rest of the world didn't exist. There was no yesterday, no tomorrow, only this moment . . .

His strong, skilful hands caressed her passionately, arousing sensations she could not control. She arched her back as she pressed against him, moaning softly at the rising ecstasy within her . . .

'Nicole; I'm not going to take you like this.' Alexander's voice was throatily urgent as he gazed tenderly into her eyes.

She stiffened in his arms; how could she behave like this? What must he think . . . ?

'It's all right my darling.' He pressed his mouth against her hair. 'I don't want to lead you astray without your full consent. Will you marry me?'

Nicole stared at the green-hazel eyes in bewilderment, unable to speak.

He chuckled softly. 'People *do* get married, you know. That's what makes the world go round.'

'Yes, but not people like *you*!' The words came out in a rush as her voice came back.

He laughed. 'And why not?'

'Because you're—*you*.' She turned away so that he couldn't see her tears, but he pulled her back against his chest.

'I don't know what you've got against me, but I'm going to find out. And I demand an answer.' He kissed her again, this time with an intimate urgency that compelled her to respond. The whole of her being was screaming yes, oh yes, I want you, Alexander Capodistrias, for better or worse . . .

There was a loud knocking on the door. 'Nicole, are you in there?'

Hurriedly she pulled the robe round her and stood up. 'It sounds like Nick.' She ran over to the door, smoothing down her ruffled hair.

'Thank goodness you're here.' The young doctor

stepped inside out of the rain.

'Oh, Nick, I'm terribly sorry, I've left your coat on the yacht. You see . . .' Nicole began.

'It doesn't matter—there's been a shipwreck outside the harbour. The cruise liner ran into difficulties and they were trying to return here when they ran aground on some rocks. They're bringing the casualties in now . . .' He sounded breathless, as if he'd been running.

'We'll come at once!' Alexander prepared to take charge of the situation as he leapt to his feet.

'I ought to dress first,' Nicole said sheepishly.

Alexander smiled lovingly at her. 'Join us as soon as you can, darling. I need you.'

Nick looked at the happy pair and grinned. 'Do I take it congratulations are in order?'

'Not yet.' Alexander gave a wistful sigh. 'The lady hasn't answered my question . . .'

'Be off with you—I want to put my uniform on,' Nicole chided.

'Yes, Sister,' Alexander chanted dutifully. 'Come on, Nick.'

Nicole's fingers trembled as she attempted to fasten the buttons on her dress, and the net cap almost defeated her. He had asked her to marry him! She took a deep breath. Concentrate, girl! You're no good to the patients like this.

She forced her attention on the emergency as she hurried down the corridor to Casualty. White-faced survivors, wrapped in blankets, huddled together in every part of the room. Some had minor injuries—cuts, bruises—and all were suffering from shock.

'See if you can wake Maria,' Nicole said to Dominic, who had been ferrying the survivors in from the wreck. 'We need lots of hot drinks.'

'And then bring the X-ray equipment in here,'

Alexander called from one of the cubicles.

'Do you want any help?' She went in to see him, her legs weak as she watched him fix a temporary splint to the patient.

'Hold this, will you.' He was his old, brusque, thoroughly professional self, but she didn't mind. She loved him all the more for his commitment and dedication.

The young man stirred on the stretcher and groaned.

'Pethidine, Sister,' Alexander said, without looking up from his task.

'Yes, sir.' She hurried away to fetch a syringe.

'I'm going to do temporary splints on the orthopaedic patients, and then we can work through the plastering together,' he told her when she returned.

She nodded. 'Good idea. There's a pregnant woman out there. Nick wants you to take a look. She's gone into labour.'

He drew in his breath. 'Why do heavily pregnant women go on cruises?'

'She's only seven months.'

'Well, I'd better go and see her.'

The young woman stared up at them from the stretcher with frightened eyes. 'I won't lose my baby, will I, Doctor?'

'We'll do all we can,' Alexander replied calmly. 'I'm going to have you moved along to Obstetrics. It's quieter along there. I'll come and examine you in a few minutes. Sister will see you into bed.'

He went back to the patient with the fractured femur, leaving Nicole to soothe the expectant mum. Dominic pushed the trolley into the corridor for her.

'In here, please. Thanks, Dominic.' She glanced at his windswept hair. 'What's it like out on the sea?'

'Never seen anything like it? It's the worst storm in living memory. I hope your friends are all right.'

She frowned. 'Which friends?'

'The people on the yacht. I saw them heading out of the harbour when I was bringing in some of the survivors. They must be mad!'

CHAPTER TWELVE

DAWN broke on a scene resembling the aftermath of a battle. Every inch of available floor space had been used to accommodate a makeshift bed. All the rooms and corridors were full of patients requiring medical help, and the entire staff of the hospital struggled to cope with the emergency. It was almost too much for Sister Croney.

'I'm not as young as I was,' she muttered as she carried a bowl of water to the delivery table.

Alexander glanced at Nicole over the top of his mask, his eyes showing amusement at the admission. 'You're doing fine; we couldn't manage without you. Wipe her forehead, again, please. It's so hot under these lights.'

'Another contraction starting . . .' Nicole removed her hand from the patient's abdomen.

'Push now, my dear. Good. Well done . . . almost there . . .'

Nicole watched, fascinated, as the wonder of birth unfolded once more. This is where it had all started —Alexander and I—bringing a new life into the world. But this one is so much easier—no complications here; a perfectly straightforward delivery at thirty-six weeks. Once the young woman had confessed that she was actually eight months—not seven—some of the tension had gone.

'I put my dates back a bit, Sister,' she had whimpered. 'We'd had this holiday booked such a long time. And my mum had promised to look after our little girl. I never thought I'd go into labour. You see they wouldn't have let me come on the cruise if they'd known I was so far advanced.'

'Don't worry, Sharon. Just concentrate on your deep breathing. You're going to be fine.' Nicole had held the patient's hand and talked to her soothingly until they reached the final stage.

'It's a boy!' Alexander handed the bawling scrap of humanity to his mother.

'Oh Doctor, he's beautiful. Thank you; thank you, so much. I wanted a boy . . . oh, you're so clever!'

Alexander laughed. 'You're the clever one, bringing a healthy baby into the world. Would you like your husband to come in now?'

'Oh, yes please; how is he?'

The poor husband had refused to be present at the birth. He was still suffering from seasickness, and had been more trouble than his wife. He came into the room, looking round apprehensively at the awesome equipment.

'What is it, Sharon?' His eyes widened as he looked at the tiny crinkled face of the baby.

'It's a boy,' she whispered.

The young father beamed happily. 'That's great!' He leaned down to kiss his wife.

Alexander looked across at Nicole, his eyes full of love and tenderness. 'When you've finished off in here, could you switch to Orthopaedics? I'm going there now.'

She nodded. 'I'll come as soon as I can.'

Impulsively he reached across and squeezed her hand. 'We'll be able to talk later.'

Sister Croney watched the surgeon walk away. There's something going on between those two, she thought, and it looks serious . . .

When the mother and baby had been settled into bed,

Nicole went along to Reception to check that things were running smoothly. Maria was serving early morning drinks, helped by Dominic and Stavros. The young drug addict had begged to be allowed to do something. 'I get so bored doing nothing,' was his plaintive cry. Alexander had decided it would be therapeutic for him to feel useful, and from the big smile on his face as he handed a cup of coffee to one of the survivors, he had been right.

'Everything okay, Dominic?'

'No problem, Sister. I've got a good assistant. I think we should put him on the payroll.'

Stavros looked suddenly shy. 'I've always wanted to be a doctor, but all those exams—and the cost of training . . .'

'You could do it, Stavros—if you really wanted to,' Dominic encouraged. 'Look at me; my father has no money, but I told Alexander I wanted to be a doctor, and he said if I worked hard he would help me. He reviews all my reports and then pays my expenses, when he sees I've worked. Next month I'm going to London. He'd do the same for you if you were really serious. That man's a saint . . .'

Nicole hurried away before she heard any more. Where had she been when that phrase was used before? Ah yes; Zoe had said it. She shivered, remembering her misgivings. We've got to have that talk!

She met up with him again in Orthopaedics.

'More bandages, Sister,' he said tersely. 'Take over from Nurse Stangos, please.'

Nicole plunged her hands into the plaster of Paris water and lifted out a bandage for the surgeon. He winked as he took it from her. 'I just want you near me,' he whispered softly. 'Don't go, will you?'

'Not until you've finished, sir.' Their eyes locked in a

conspiratorial gaze, before he turned all his attention on
the patient.

It was midday before they dared to escape together.
Sister Croney was the one who pointed out that they'd
had no sleep.

'You'll fall asleep standing up if you don't take a
break, Alexander,' she remonstrated in a kindly tone.
'And take Sister Langley with you. She looks dead on
her feet.'

Nicole laughed happily as they ran down the steps to
the boat. 'If I didn't know her better, I'd say Sister
Croney was trying to matchmake.'

'I'd say you were right first time. Don't underestimate
the old dear. She's a romantic soul at heart.'

'I still don't see why we have to go all the way round to
Symborio. I mean, we'll have to go back in a couple of
hours . . .'

'Quiet woman.' He scooped her into his arms and
deposited her in the silver boat, oblivious to the curious
onlookers.

As they headed out of the harbour she couldn't take
her eyes from the tall frame at the helm. The wind was
ruffling his dark hair, making him look casual and
boyish. His jaw was set in a determined line, and he
looked deep in thought.

Don't tell me anything I don't want to know, she
prayed fervently. I hope I was wrong.

The white, crenellated façade of the Capodistrias
house came into view, and she took a deep breath. She
had vowed never to come here again, but today it
seemed inviting in the hot sunlight. The storm had
subsided, leaving a tranquil calm on the water that
belied the tempestuous night.

Demetrius came to meet them as they reached the

courtyard. 'What a pleasant surprise! You'll stay for lunch?'

'Of course; but first we need some time to ourselves. I'll take Nicole to my room, so we can be alone. Tell Eirene we don't want to be disturbed,' Alexander told his father.

Demetrius smiled happily. 'Whatever you say, my boy.'

They climbed the ornate staircase together. Nicole glanced at the lavish portraits of the Capodistrias' ancestors staring down at her; centuries of history she knew nothing about. But then, she knew nothing about the present Capodistrias. At last she was to find out . . .

Alexander opened the door to his room, and Nicole walked over the thick wool pile carpet to the balcony. She felt intensely nervous. Why had he brought her here? Couldn't he have said what he had to say back at the hospital?

She felt his arms around her waist, and she turned to meet his kiss. It was soft, gentle, without the agonising urgency of yesterday. 'I love you,' he whispered, holding her against him as if she were a delicate flower that he was afraid of crushing.

She looked up into his handsome, rugged face, not wanting to shatter the rapport between them, but desperate to allay her fears. Where should she start? 'Tell me about yesterday—on the yacht.'

'You were marvellous, catching on so quickly.' He gazed down in admiration. 'If you'd started to argue, we'd have been lost.'

'Why?'

'Because the Greek knew I was on to them.'

Nicole's eyes narrowed in bewilderment. 'I don't know what you're talking about.'

He smiled patiently. 'I'd better start at the beginning,

I think. Come over here.' He took her hand and led her over to the bed.

'Alexander, if you think you can get round me . . .'

'I'll do the talking. Just lie here and listen.' He swung her into his arms and laid her gently on the counterpane.

She lay very still, hardly daring to breathe. 'Before you start your explanation, I feel I must tell you that I saw you one day, in the Oceanis, when you took a package from the African.' Her accusation came out in a guilty rush.

'So that was what was worrying you. Now I understand.' He lifted himself on to his elbow beside her and looked down at her with a deep tenderness in his eyes.

'I wish *I* did . . .' Nicole said.

'Hush, little one.' He brushed his lips lightly across hers, causing a feeling of limpness in every limb.

'My nephew Marcus became addicted to heroin after his father was killed in a car crash.' Alexander's voice was deadly serious and the pain showed in his expression. 'At first, Vanessa didn't realise what was going on. When she found out, it was too late. He took an overdose and died on his eighteenth birthday.'

Tears welled into Nicole's eyes. 'I'm sorry; I had no idea.'

'I volunteered to help the drug squad as medical advisor. We were tipped off about a drugs ring operating from the coast of Turkey, and I was asked to come out here. It was a wrench to leave my work in the UK, but I wanted to do something to avenge the needless death of my nephew. And I had the obvious advantage of being a native here.'

She reached out a hand in sympathy. The grief he felt for Marcus was etched on his face. He raised her hand to his lips, too overcome by emotion to continue.

'So you came out to Ceres on an errand of mercy . . .' Nicole finished for him.

'I came out to smash the drug smugglers, to stop the endless waste of young lives.' His voice was strong again as he talked about his mission on the island. 'I suspected Mike was involved, but I didn't know to what extent until I delved deeper. In fact, he was the ringleader we were looking for.'

'*Mike* was?' Nicole gazed at Alexander in disbelief. 'But he seemed such an innoccuous sort of man. I had my doubts about Fiona and the rest of the crew—' She broke off suddenly. 'His hair was dyed—did you know that?'

Alexander smiled. 'I noticed it when he was in hospital. He's wanted by the police for absconding bail. They showed me his photograph in their files. He looks quite different when he has dark hair and a moustache, but I was able to identify him. That's why I flew back to England to the so-called conference. The African crew member had given me some heroin, as a sample. It was risky, because I thought I might get picked up by the customs before I could reach the drug squad. As it was, I was able to advise them about setting up the operation to nail them.'

'But they've gone! Dominic saw them leaving Ceres harbour last night, in the middle of the storm.'

He grinned. 'Don't worry. We know all about that. They've been under surveillance ever since I got back. I got a message to say that they were riding out the storm on the Turkish coast. As soon as they reach England they'll be picked up. We know exactly which little cove they're heading for.'

'So your father's heart attack was just an excuse to get out here, I presume?'

'Yes; he wasn't very convincing, was he? He's as fit as

a fiddle. Never had a day's illness in his life. He can't wait to get back to work again, and the patients at the pharmacy will be delighted to see him.'

'And Sister Croney, too!' Nicole smiled wickedly.

'Oh yes; she never gives up hope.' He reached across as if to pull her towards him.

'Just one more question,' Nicole said. 'Why did the Greek say he recognised your voice?'

'He heard me talking to the African one night, when I'd gone to the yacht to see what I could find. That was when we had to arrange another meeting—in the Oceanis, when you saw me.'

'I also saw you sneaking off to the yacht that night, and I won't tell you what I suspected!'

'You thought I was having an affair with Fiona, didn't you?' This time he caught her in his arms.

'Something like that,' she confessed.

'And were you jealous?' Alexander was laughing at the expression on her face.

'Of course I wasn't—well, maybe just a little bit. What did annoy me was the way you put up with her dreadful nursing.'

'I hated that too, believe me, but I was sure she was qualified. The papers she showed me must have been perfect forgeries. I thought she was taking longer than usual to adapt, and I needed to worm my way into her confidence and extract as much valuable information from her as I could. When I was in London, I checked with the General Nursing Council—they'd never heard of her. I knew I'd got to get rid of her, so I asked her to meet me for lunch and bring her 'references' with her. She didn't come; that was when I invited you to fill in . . .'

'Well, thanks very much . . .' Nicole began indignantly, but his lips silenced her protest. He kissed her hungrily, passionately, as if his life depended upon it, and she met his highly charged emotions with her own. She wanted to drown in the ecstasy of his embrace, to abandon her body in the all consuming delirium of their love. The feel of his hands on her skin sent shivers of delight tingling down her spine. This was the destiny she had awaited all her life; to love and be loved in a unity of body and spirit that could never be separated. They would merge into one person, inseparable for all time . . .

She stirred in his arms, languorously, like a cat that has just had a saucer of cream. Alexander had fallen asleep, his hair in rich curls over his forehead. Nicole gazed at him lovingly, the man she would marry. He opened his eyes and smiled.

'So, what's your answer?' His voice was low and husky with the warmth of consummation.

'What was the question?' she teased. 'No, Alexander, stop it.' She pulled away. 'I want to hear you say it again.'

'Will you marry me?'

She looked into the smiling face. 'I think I'd better. You'll have to make an honest woman of me now.'

'And the sooner the better. We'll be married in the little white church above the harbour—Ayios Athanasios.'

'But will you have to go back to England, now that your work here is finished?'

'On the contrary—my work here has only just begun. I'm going to expand the hospital and start a treatment clinic for drug addicts. I intend to take patients of any nationality. My colleagues in England will send their patients to be cured here. It's an ideal spot to kick drug addiction.' His eyes shone with excitement as he outlined his plans.

'Stavros wants to be cured,' Nicole said softly. 'He'd like to be a doctor . . .'

'There's no reason why he shouldn't be. He's an intelligent boy. If he'll work as hard as Dominic, I'll see him through medical school.' He kissed her lightly on the tip of her nose. 'And now, Mrs Capodistrias, we'd better go and tell Father the good news before we go back to hospital.'

'How do you feel about married women working?' she asked shyly.

'I've no objection to my wife working before she has children—so that gives you at least nine months . . .'

Nicole aimed a pillow at his head. He ducked and caught her in his arms. 'I just want you to be happy, my love. And as long as you can find time to give me a few sons, and a sprinkling of daughters as beautiful as their mother . . .'

'I'll need your help, Doctor . . .'

4 Doctor Nurse Romances
FREE

Coping with the daily tragedies and ordeals of a busy hospital, and sharing the satisfaction of a difficult job well done, people find themselves unexpectedly drawn together. Mills & Boon Doctor Nurse Romances capture perfectly the excitement, the intrigue and the emotions of modern medicine, that so often lead to overwhelming and blissful love. By becoming a regular reader of Mills & Boon Doctor Nurse Romances you can enjoy SIX superb new titles every two months plus a whole range of special benefits: your very own personal membership card, a free newsletter packed with recipes, competitions, bargain book offers, plus big cash savings.

**AND an Introductory FREE GIFT for YOU.
Turn over the page for details.**

**Fill in and send this coupon back today
and we'll send you**

4 Introductory
Doctor Nurse Romances yours to keep
FREE

At the same time we will reserve a
subscription to Mills & Boon
Doctor Nurse Romances for you. Every
two months you will receive the latest
6 new titles, delivered direct to your door.
You don't pay extra for delivery. Postage and
packing is always completely Free.
There is no obligation or commitment –
you receive books only for
as long as you want to.

**It's easy! Fill in the coupon below and return it to
MILLS & BOON READER SERVICE, FREEPOST, P.O. BOX 236,
CROYDON, SURREY CR9 9EL.**

- -

FREE BOOKS CERTIFICATE

**To: Mills & Boon Reader Service, FREEPOST, P.O. Box 236,
Croydon, Surrey CR9 9EL.**

Please send me, free and without obligation, four Dr. Nurse Romances, and reserve a Reader
Service Subscription for me. If I decide to subscribe I shall receive, following my free parcel of
books, six new Dr. Nurse Romances every two months for £6.60 , post and packing free. If I
decide not to subscribe, I shall write to you within 10 days. The free books are mine to keep in
any case. I understand that I may cancel my subscription at any time simply by writing to you. I
am over 18 years of age.
Please write in BLOCK CAPITALS.

Name _____

Address _____

_____

_____ Postcode _____

SEND NO MONEY — TAKE NO RISKS

*Mills & Boon reserve the right to exercise discretion in granting
membership. If price changes are necessary you will be notified.*
   You may be mailed with other offers as a result of this
6DN *application. Offer expires 31st December 1986.*

EPDO